ALSO BY JOSEPH STONE

A DARK FANTASY NOVEL

ALIVE

THE GHOST OF CAMBRIA

BOOK ONE

JOSEPH STONE

SILVER LION
PUBLISHING

Editing by Jerrica McDowell

ISBN: 9781707960750

DEDICATION

FOR TRISTA FAE LIPE,
a remarkable woman and beloved friend.

Here is a dark story about science and fear,
written just for you.

Nothing is so painful to the human mind as a great and sudden change.

MARY WOLLSTONECRAFT SHELLEY,
FRANKENSTEIN OR THE MODERN PROMETHEUS

CHAPTER ONE

"THANK YOU FOR YOUR CONSIDERATION, SIR," TONY said, beaming a grateful smile.

After shaking his hand, Richard Cole watched the smart young man leave down the front pathway to the street. He didn't take his eyes off the kid until Tony had driven away in his older blue pickup truck. Richard was too excited by what Tony had just offered him. It was only a blind adherence to standard business protocols that kept him from agreeing to hire the guy right on the spot. Instead, Richard promised to let Tony know once he had time to consider his proposal.

But there was nothing more to consider.

Richard had lived in his Cambia home for five years now. He and his wife, Margaret, had moved here from San Diego, bent on retreating to their favorite sleepy town on the central California coast. As their only daughter had completed graduate school, there was nothing more to keep Richard from cashing in and starting his retirement.

And he'd done it!

Moving here had given Richard the most excellent feeling

of accomplishment, on par only with raising his beautiful daughter to adulthood and seeing her flourish.

Though Margaret had talked him into buying a larger retirement house than they needed, some four bedrooms in total, Richard had managed to make it work. They wouldn't be able to travel as much as their friends would like, but he and his wife were both homebodies. The house would need updating one day, but that, too, meant very little to them. Living among the soaring pine trees, only a five-minute walk to the pristine surf, was everything they had dreamed of together. Who cared if the kitchen didn't have those granite slab countertops people craved these days? They intended to spend very little of their new life cooking for anyone.

But their dream soon became a nightmare. Margaret was diagnosed with inoperable cancer. Richard's medical insurance was costlier in retirement than when he was employed. Worse, they had never considered how expensive dying from cancer might be, and their provider didn't cover the cutting-edge treatments offered to extend Margaret's life.

Richard's first inclination was to sell the house. He would need to update parts of their home to sell it fast, but what of it?

Margaret, however, would not leave.

As she became weaker and the pain of the tumors grew, Richard hadn't the heart to make her suffer through even one more moment of grief.

Eventually, he took money out of the house to settle the final expenses. It was just enough to cover the last hospital and hospice payments once they had released Margaret from her agony. In his despair, finding himself in this large, empty house with only the most painful memories wherever he looked, Richard knew he needed to do something. When he applied for a part-time professorship at the local university, it was to fill his days with the noise of life more than anything. Richard sought any reason to be away from the silent memories of her pain. But he also knew it was the only way to pay off the equity mortgage and afford the updates needed to sell the home.

It would take time to carry out, but time was all Richard had left now.

And then, this morning, something unexpected happened. A bright, motivated young man named Tony De Luca had visited the house to ask about renovating it all by himself.

"I want to be more than a carpenter," Tony explained with passion in his voice. "I want to be an artisan."

Making Richard's home shine brighter than ever was the type of break Tony craved. With the rebirth of the house, the young man could create a photo portfolio that would open the types of doors he needed to ensure his career and dreams.

Tony would do the work in his own time, which would take years. He would take the house apart, room by room, and replace almost everything with the most exquisite craftsmanship imaginable. But Tony would charge Richard nothing for his services. He only needed money for professional plumbers and electricians besides the building materials.

In any other scenario, Richard would need to save for years before he could contract the work, and it would never come close to the quality this kid promised. Tony would restore the house from nine to five while Richard lectured at the local university. By the time he cleared the note, Richard could sell the house at a phenomenal price and start his retirement again in a more reasonable dwelling.

The idea set Richard's mind alight, and he danced up the stairs to the bedroom to draw a bath and relax. The exuberant man carried a large glass of Tobin James' Fat Boy Zinfandel, his favorite red. Today's news called for the perfect glass of wine and a fun espionage novel on his e-reader to celebrate.

Richard had only just moved back into the primary bedroom. Weeks after he and his wife moved into the house, Richard had taken another bedroom to give Margaret space while she suffered from her illness. After her death, Richard avoided the room for a year. But in time, after a heavy season of grieving, Richard made peace with his wife's death and reestablished himself in the master bedroom. To his surprise, being back in the room had kept the beautiful parts of her memory close to him.

Richard opened the tap and let the water run warm before closing the tub's drain. He poured bath salt in the water, a remedy that worked best on his arthritis, which often flared in his right hip.

Turning to undress, Richard realized a young man stood in the bathroom doorway. At first, he thought Tony had returned to the house, but realized the man was a stranger. He was taller than Richard with a solid build and dark, wavy black hair. His steel-blue eyes set stared out from under a furrowed brow. The intruder wore a heavy crewneck sweater made of dark gray wool and brown corduroy pants, which seemed worn at the knees. Barefoot, he stared at Richard in silence for several agonizing moments before the older man overcame the shock of the confrontation and gathered the wherewithal to speak.

"What are you doing here, son?" Richard asked calmly. "This is my home."

He thought the man's face was familiar but couldn't remember where he'd seen it.

"You should leave now," said Richard, again calmly. "There's nothing here for you to take. Do you need help?"

The silent man's chest moved, and he raised his head, drawing breath as if he were about to speak, but no sound came.

With one fine blow, an invisible force pushed Richard back violently onto the hard tile of the bathroom floor. His head hit the edge of the cast iron bathtub with a painful thud, and the lights in the room went dark.

Richard couldn't see, nor hear, nor move.

After a few moments, there was nothing at all.

CHAPTER TWO

"ARE YOU GOING TO MAKE ME TAKE MEDICINE? WILL that make it stop?" the anxious girl asked.

Kristen Cole sat in her office across from Mona, a nineteen-year-old college student assigned for psychological appraisal. The girl's parents had admitted her into Sharp Memorial Hospital after Mona's dorm mate, Jessica, called them in a panic.

Mona attended a house party last night. It had been Jessica's idea—a simple outing to lift the girl's spirits. Mona had become insufferable after breaking up with her boyfriend and falling into depression. At the party, the two girls had spent hours playing games and drinking with dozens of friends and peers. Losing track of her roommate at some point, Jessica searched the house and came across Mona sitting in a dark, unoccupied bedroom. When Jessica flicked the switch to light the room, she realized Mona was alone and talking to a photograph of a man framed on the bed's side table. When Jessica spoke to the girl, Mona carried on with the bizarre conversation as if she couldn't hear her friend calling her name. No matter how vigorously Jessica shook Mona, the girl continued the delusional discussion.

"From all you've told me, I don't think that'll be necessary," Kristen answered gently, hoping that her warm smile would place the girl at ease.

"My mom said you'd give me pills to make me feel better," the girl replied, almost as if instructing Kristen to give them to her. "She says I'm over-stressed with school and all."

"Do you think that's what happened to you?" Kristen asked.

Mona didn't answer the question. Tears threatened to return, and she looked away from the psychologist.

Kristen didn't push the girl for an answer.

"Mom says I should ask for Xanax," said Mona, impatience and desperation coloring her voice.

"I don't prescribe medication," Kristen clarified, "and I wouldn't suggest your physician allow you to have it. Xanax is not a reasonable solution for you. It would be a Band-Aid, but it would come at too a high price."

The mood stabilizer Mona requested had become alarmingly prevalent over the past decade. Bordering on an epidemic, physicians prescribed Xanax if a patient so much as experienced a bad day. Unfortunately, it had become rare for a physician to bother with a remedial psychological evaluation to determine if a patient's condition warranted the drug.

Kristen dropped her eyes to review the PHQ-9 test processed by the nurse when Mona was first administered to the hospital. Nothing on the document showed Jessica suffered from something worth risking the side effects of psychotropic medication. She hadn't attempted suicide, nor even contemplated it. Mona's depression had been going on for less than a month. She hadn't used recreational substances to cope, short of the juvenile blending of Jell-O with cheap alcohol, known as 'Scooby-Snacks,' served at the party. The closest indicator present was that Mona had recently experienced a breakup with her boyfriend.

"What's the name of the guy you broke up with?" asked Kristen.

"Josh," the girl answered hesitantly.

"And how long had you been seeing Josh?"

"We were together since the end of freshman year," the girl responded, her voice filled with wary distrust. "But we've known each other since high school."

"Did you date him back when you were in high school?" the psychologist asked.

"A little bit," she answered after a pause. "Not exclusively until this past April," Mona added.

"So, you dated for four months, but you'd had a crush on Josh for years. Is that a fair statement?"

"Yes," Mona acknowledged, her eyes searching the wall for anything to stare at, avoiding the psychologist's face.

"Was Josh your first boyfriend? Your first *real* boyfriend?"

The girl nodded her head silently.

"The two of you separated on bad terms?"

Again, the girl nodded her reply.

"Did he cheat on you?"

Mona didn't answer, but the silence was a loud enough confirmation.

"And he was the first guy you had sex with?"

Tears broke on Mona's face as she looked at Kristen with a forced smile. She brought a crumpled tissue to her eyes to catch them before they fell. The girl had begun the session with tears of fear, but now they came from the miserable embarrassment of sharing intimacies with a stranger.

Kristen had trained herself not to cry in front of her

patients, an accomplishment few non-professionals could understand or appreciate. Crying had the effect of validating a patient's concerns, which was often counterproductive.

After such focused training on the skill of empathy, it was a test of will for the psychologist to avoid weeping during a counseling session. Empathy placed Kristen directly into a patient's mind so she could experience the same emotions as the patient. It was a method meant to achieve increased psychological understanding. As a result, Kristen's empathy muscles were so over-developed that they doomed her to feel a patient's emotions even more sharply than she could feel her own. And Mona's tears now cut through Kristen like a scalding knife, forcing her to recall how painful her first breakup was.

But that wasn't something she could share with the girl.

"Understand that no one is ever going to know about this conversation," Kristen whispered. "My only purpose is to help you through this, and I'm on your side. I'll never betray your confidence in me."

"I feel like an idiot," the girl wept.

"God no," said Kristen, her eyebrows furrowed sharply. "Getting out of your first love unscathed is almost unheard of. Most of us land pretty hard. What concerns me is the way you got up from your fall. Let me tell you a story."

"This happened to you?" Mona asked.

"Yes, but that story won't do much for you," Kristen assured her with a caring frown. "I want to tell you a little story about neurotransmitters."

Mona stared with confusion in her eyes.

"We have a *brain*, and we have a *mind*—and the two are different. The brain is the large spongy grey thing behind our eyeballs. You've seen a picture in a biology class by now. It's our central computer, regulating every part of our body, from our heartbeat to our breathing. The mind is something else, but unquestionably linked to the brain. When we stub our toe, our foot sends information to the brain, and then the brain warns our mind that we hurt ourselves. Do you know how it does that? The brain sends neurotransmitters that result in the sensation of pain. It does this so we will stop and pay attention to our toe. It wants us to baby our foot for a minute and make sure it's not broken. The brain is trying to keep us healthy and safe, so it focuses our mind's attention on something threatening, like breaking a toe.

"On the other hand, we understand very little about the mind. But the mind is... Mona, or Kristen," she said, bringing her hand to her chest, "or Beyoncé, or your mom. Our mind is *us*. All our thoughts, dreams, fears, knowledge—everything we feel or know—that's what the mind is. Some people will tell you the mind is your spirit or soul. Others think it's something extraordinary the brain creates to increase our ability to survive in our environment. What we know for sure is that the mind is dependent upon and influenced by the brain. Are you with me?"

"My brain told me to cry?" asked Mona, a confused expression on her tired face.

Kristen repressed a giggle.

"Close!" she said, lighting up her eyes. "Most times, you'd be right. But sometimes, the roles are reversed, and the *mind* influences the *brain*. When our mind feels sad for any reason —whether we get into a fight, or our dog dies, or a lover betrays us—our mind influences our brain. The most common response to that influence is that we start to cry. But it doesn't make much sense, does it? The whole thing is weird if you think about it. Why does water pick those inconvenient moments to spring out of our eyes? Why would our mind

11

influence our brain to send neurotransmitters to instruct our tear ducts to make more tears? What good does that do?"

Mona blinked as if Kristen finally had her attention.

"It turns out that when our mind feels emotional pain, our brain misinterprets the sadness as a physical threat, so it instructs our tear ducts to make more water to protect our eyes from the perceived danger."

Mona gave an incredulous stare at the psychologist, both confused by the purpose of the woman's story and annoyed that she'd inundated her with a useless science lecture.

"What's your point?" the impatient girl asked.

"I'm almost there," Kristen promised. "There's a different neurotransmitter for every single action the brain instructs the body to do, even loving. When a woman gives birth, her brain sends neurotransmitters to flood her with oxytocin. That's a chemical that makes her fall in love with the baby. The mom gets another powerful shot of oxytocin into her bloodstream whenever the baby cries.

"Think about it. If your roommate woke you up at three in the morning, you'd probably tell her to shut up, right? You wouldn't get out of bed and run to hold and comfort her, would you?"

"That's different," Mona exhaled. "Jessica isn't my baby. She's an inconsiderate noisy bitch."

"Exactly!" cheered Kristen. "Now imagine if Jessica belonged to you—if you had a legal obligation to care for her. What if Jessica didn't speak, if she didn't understand a word you said but was reliant on you for food or diaper changes, or bathing? Can you imagine how annoying that would become —not getting more than a couple of hours of sleep at a time because Jessica kept waking you up to attend to her? I'm not saying I would drop Jessica off on someone's doorstep, but I might consider it. Wouldn't you?"

"Within the first hour," Mona conceded.

"That's where the neurotransmitters come to the rescue. You might say the brain wants us to succeed. It will do anything to make sure we're safe and productive. So, it floods a mother with oxytocin so she'll fall in love with her baby. Mothers often develop a bond so inexplicably strong that they won't hesitate to place the baby's needs before their own.

"Have you ever attempted to tell the mother of a newborn that her baby is somehow imperfect? I wouldn't try it unless you want to watch her turn into a ninja assassin on you."

Mona laughed, despite herself.

"I'm serious," Kristen pressed, "she'll slice your head off without even thinking about it—just for looking at her baby wrong. That's how protective she is of her ugly little poo-smelling blob: irrationally protective. And that's how powerful neurotransmitters are."

"I get it," said Mona.

"Good, so then it won't surprise you that the brain has other weapons to help you succeed in its arsenal."

"There's one for loving your boyfriend?" smiled the girl.

"Oh, you just gave me chills. I'm so proud of you!" Kristen raised her voice with approval, shifting excitedly in her seat. "Yes, there's a neurotransmitter whose sole purpose is to make you fall in love with your boyfriend. The mind sees a boy you like, and the brain sends neurotransmitters to flood you with a similar chemical. Except this one makes you desire that boy in every way imaginable. You know now what that sensation feels like, right? Like you're walking on air, like the sun rises and sets in his pants. Where every stupid thing he does makes you laugh and love him more. You find yourself doing anything for him. Even the most questionable stuff you'd never consider doing in your right mind."

"What's that chemical called?"

"Phenethylamine," Kristen answered, repeating the word a second time to break up the five syllables for the girl. "It's called PEA for short."

"So, it wasn't real? I didn't really love him?"

"No, you loved him. That's just it; you had little choice in the matter because the chemical supported your love. The real problem is you were only a few months into loving him, so the brain hadn't finished drugging you. PEA levels only dissipate after a good two years of romantic love, by which time we have learned to love our boyfriend the way a rational adult loves another person. The way you love your best friend or a sibling. We can't trust someone after four months, not enough to want a baby with them. Trust is earned over a long time. You were just starting with Josh, but your love affair ended unexpectedly, and that's why you're sitting in that chair today."

"What do you mean? I ran out of neurotransmitters?"

"Worse, they cut you off from the magic chemical as soon as you broke up. You were hooked on the junk, and then just like that," Kristen snapped her fingers, "your brain took it away. Cold turkey. So, all the normal pain you felt—the betrayal, the insecurity, the loneliness—was amplified because you didn't have the chemical high to help you through the transition."

The girl stared at Kristen, seemingly baffled by how something so simple could have happened.

"That's stupid," she declared.

"Yeah, well, not from your brain's point of view. Think about it—the only reason it fed you that chemical in the first place was so you'd fall in love with the boy. It was trying to get you to mate with him. The brain has an agenda, after all. It's trying to get you to make a baby. It wants you to procreate."

"I don't want a goddamn baby," Mona raised her voice.

"Well, your brain shares a different opinion," countered Kristen. "The blueprint for our brain is ancient. And I don't mean *human* ancient; I mean *universe* ancient. You understand how evolution works, right? The fittest species is the one that survives to reproduce. Well, billions of years later, no matter how the mind has evolved to do calculus and build skyscrapers, our brains are still coded with the primary goal of reproduction. So, while Mona might think having a baby is a dumb idea today—and she's quite right—her brain is programmed to do whatever it can to make it happen.

"Now, one of the side-effects of the chemical withdrawals we might go through are delusions. And the delusions we might experience during a PEA withdrawal can be intense because it happens at the same time we're withdrawn, not exercising, and not sleeping well. We might hear, smell, and even see things that aren't there."

"That's what happened to me?" asked Mona.

"Let's have another session in a few weeks to see your progress. But right now, you don't meet the criteria for any disorders calling for medication. You don't even come close enough for me to diagnose you as having chronic depression. If you're experiencing delusions like the one you've described, it's most likely a reaction to your sudden PEA withdrawal, paired with the other factors I mentioned."

"So, I'm a junky?" Mona scowled at her.

"Frustrating, right?" Kristen sighed.

"That's idiotic!" Mona blurted out.

"At least you know what's happened to you. And now we can take measures to prevent it from recurring."

"How?" the girl asked, again seeming anxious about the psychologist's answer.

"We use the neurotransmitters to our advantage," said

Kristen, scribbling on a small, white pad. "I told you the brain releases them to solve problems. Well, we know how to make the brain release a particular neurotransmitter that will make you feel better than any cocktail or smoke ever will."

"Chocolate?" she asked. "Like in Harry Potter?"

"Even better, though, you should make a point to eat a piece of chocolate daily. Have you ever heard of the expression fight or flight?"

"Sure, I guess."

"When we're in danger, we do one of two things: we either stand up and fight an aggressor or run away from them. The same is true for every animal in creation; the ones who survive are the most ferocious fighters or those who can run the fastest. If we run away, our body works overtime to make our legs move to save us from getting eaten. Once we escape, our brain triggers a neurotransmitter that floods us with a chemical that counteracts all the fear and anxiety that got us running. It does this so we calm down. It's taxing on our bodies to invest all that energy. The chemical makes us feel calmer and clearer, and we also experience a perfect euphoria that lasts for hours. A few shots of that stuff and a beautiful young woman won't have any trouble getting over a breakup, I promise."

Kristen twisted the pen to close it and handed her patient the small sheet of paper.

Mona read the scribbling aloud.

"Run as fast as I can for as long as I can. Rest. Repeat."

"You'll feel better than new," Kristen said.

"I already do this," Mona said with an agitated sigh. "I'm on the cross-country track team. I already know about endorphins."

"Nope, that's jogging. That's a different chemical. You only get access to the one you need at present after your heartbeat reaches a certain rate for a specific length of time. You must trick the brain into thinking you're running for your life. Hyper-sprinting."

"As fast as I can for as long as I can?"

"That's it. You said you have access to a racetrack? That'll work fine. Otherwise, you can set a treadmill to move as fast as you can keep up."

Mona stared at the paper, unsure.

"Well, I need to end our session here," said Kristen, rising from her seat to walk the girl to the door, "but I'm confident you'll feel much better as soon as you follow those steps."

Kristen extended her hand to the girl, who received it and shook it with distracted focus.

"Thank you, Doctor Cole," she said, the strength in her voice returning.

"Your very welcome, Mona," the doctor smiled through her light green eyes.

Once the door closed behind the girl, Kristen sat at her desk to type up her notes from the session. Completing the forms required to satisfy the hospital and insurance providers was a chore.

Kristen ran her hands through her red hair to move it out of her face. She usually kept it tied back at work, but she had taken a shot at blowing it out this morning. A colleague had mentioned how beautiful the vibrant color would shine and complement Kristen's light green eyes if only she'd put in the time. Though the comment had quietly incensed Kristen, she knew the woman's words hadn't been said to offer offense, and she spent time on the chore this morning.

Kristen's cell phone vibrated inside her purse on the credenza behind her, and she turned to check if it was an important call. She didn't recognize the caller, but 'San Luis Obispo' flashed above the unknown number.

"This is Doctor Cole," she answered.

"Good afternoon. Is this Kristen Cole?"

"Speaking," she said.

"Hello, this is Mark Pomeroy. I am a chancellor at Cal Poly. One of our professors has listed you as his emergency contact."

"Yes, that's my father, Richard Cole. Is everything all right?"

When the man struggled to answer, Kristen felt her pulse rise in panic.

CHAPTER THREE

"I'M AFRAID YOU'LL END UP SELLING THIS HOUSE AT A loss," Kemp said as he made his way through the kitchen.

Brian Kemp was the fourth agent Kristen had contacted yesterday, but the first to return her call with a promise to show up and offer an appraisal.

The drive to the small seaside hamlet of Cambria was always a trial for Kristen, one that ensured she only visited her parent's home twice each year. The most congested parts of the Southern California megalopolis lay between this house and her small condominium in San Diego. After requiring seven hours to drive just three hundred miles, Kristen had barely mustered enough strength to find her way to the guest room and fall into bed. She hadn't been prepared for Kemp's arrival when the doorbell woke her just before nine o'clock.

"No one has updated this kitchen in thirty years," Kemp said with undisguised dismay. "No buyer will see the property as anything but a fixer-upper—not in this neighborhood. We could let it sit for a while if you weren't in a hurry. A better price might come along, eventually. But I doubt anyone will pay over seven-fifty. I would drop it to six hundred if you need it sold within the month."

The number hit Kristen in the gut.

Of the many surprises her father's estate attorney shared with her this week, the most perplexing was that her parents took an equity mortgage out on the house. When her father retired from his practice five years ago, moving her mother from San Diego to this quiet town of six thousand souls, it was the fulfillment of his life's goal to retire in his home state. When Kristen asked why they had chosen such a large home for two people, her father had shaken his head and looked at his wife to imply Kristen already knew the answer to her question.

The following month, her mother passed away, leaving the man to face a solitary life for the first time in over forty years of marriage. Richard agreed with Kristen's eventual suggestion to sell the home but insisted he'd need to renovate it first or lose out on a significant potential return.

"That's ridiculous," said Kristen. "I looked through a few real estate apps on my pad this week—the average home price in this area is more than a million dollars."

"Almost one-point-five million on this street," Kemp answered. "The house four doors down sold for two-point-three last year. It's a larger house, but the location got them that price."

After she paid back the equity loan, Kristen would only stand to make three hundred thousand dollars on the sale. It was a large sum, but not an amount that would go far in San Diego. Even if she sold her one-bedroom condo, the combined amounts wouldn't get her into a house unless it was so far away from the coast that she might as well move to Arizona. As she'd also learned, there was little else she would inherit beyond this house. Another foolish expectation crumbled away at the realtor's words.

"If you put some money into the property," Kemp continued, "at least updated this kitchen and the bathrooms —give it a professional paint job and stage it properly—you'd do far better on the market. You could ask for more than a million if you redid the yards and improved the drive-by appeal. That's what any investor who buys it will do."

Kristen continued her silent argument, staring at the house with contempt. The Craftsman revival-styled home was built in the late seventies. Though it looked handsome enough on the outside, the interior was basic. Much of the house's finishes were inconsistent; the kitchen was a mid-eighties nightmare, the bathrooms received a minor resurfacing in the nineties, and it's obvious they did the updates on the cheap. The few examples of the popular Craftsman style that adorned the two-story home were mostly in the living and dining rooms.

"How much would you spend on a renovation, knowing you intended only to sell it?"

"Two hundred and fifty thousand dollars," Kemp answered resolutely.

Kristen couldn't hide a sharp scowl at the man.

"I understand," he said, raising his hands in melodramatic defense, "but that's what I would spend. You could hide almost everything wrong here, at least well enough that folks would pay. Not for top dollar, perhaps, but double what you'd get for it today."

Kristen ran her anxious hands through her light red hair. She found it was still wild from having no time to run a brush through it before stumbling to the front door to receive Kemp.

"It's not just that I don't have the money, Brian. What you're suggesting would take months to finish," she said.

"At least six months," the agent shot the number to be clear. "I can steer you toward a firm that'll do a good job for you, but that's how long you're looking at and how much it will cost."

Kristen resisted the entire notion of such a project. She couldn't rely upon much more than a couple of weeks' leave from the medical facility, and she couldn't hope to get a renovation done without being in Cambria several days a week.

"I live in San Diego, Brian," she said with finality. "I can't make that work."

"You wouldn't need to be here all the time. You could have a project manager handle it for you. What decisions couldn't make over FaceTime?" asked Kemp, pointing to the iPhone on the kitchen island beside her purse.

"A site manager would cost even more money I don't have," she returned.

"It would," he admitted, "but no one does work for free. It's still a reasonable option."

Kristen heard the words escape her lips well before her mind had reached its conclusion.

"Who do you recommend I call?" she asked.

Kemp couldn't repress a victorious smile at her concession.

"I'll forward you two contacts as soon as I get back to the office," he promised. "And I'll be ready to get you a serious offer for this place in six months."

Kristen nodded with reservations, still uncertain of what she was agreeing to.

Kemp tapped her information into his cellphone display, fleshing out the contact he'd begun with her name and number yesterday. He let the young woman verify his entry before shaking her hand to thank her.

Kristen walked him to the door and onto the front porch, where she watched Kemp descend the simple concrete and red brick pathway to the street.

As the realtor arrived on the sidewalk, Kristen saw him pause to speak to another man passing by. The stranger motioned as if he meant to walk up and visit the house, and she wondered if he was another realtor arriving a minute too late. Kemp nodded and looked back at the house to Kristen, who stopped herself from returning inside.

The young man proceeded up the steep walkway trek as Kemp sat in his white Mercedes sedan to drive away.

"Good morning," the stranger called from about thirty feet away.

As he came closer, Kristen could see the guy was even younger than she'd first suspected. His skin bore the silky sheen that only someone in their early twenties still produced. Underneath was a light olive complexion that made his chiseled jaw unmistakable. His athletic build filled out a black Polo shirt that seemed far too old a style for someone so young.

"Is Mister Cole at home?" he asked with a polite grin.

"No, I'm sorry," Kristen answered awkwardly, lowering her voice. "He passed away last week."

The light all but extinguished in the young man's brown eyes. He struggled to exhale, processing the unexpected news.

"I'm his daughter, Kristen. Did you know him?" she asked gently, seeing the man's failed attempt to mask his distress.

"I'm so sorry," he answered after a pause, appearing to collect his focus with difficulty. "No, I didn't know Richard that well, but I hadn't heard from him in a couple of weeks, so I thought I would check in on him."

The young man paused again, seeming to take another moment to gather his thoughts before continuing.

"I'm sorry," he said again with a slight jerk of his head, "my name is Tony. I submitted a proposal to your father for work he wanted done on this house."

"Oh, I see," answered Kristen, moving down the stairs to stand beside Tony. "Dad had an accident last week—he fell and hit his head. He worked part-time lecturing at CalPoly, and they called me when he didn't show up for work. The police found him…"

She realized her voice had wavered. Kristen had cried for hours during the drive up the coast yesterday, listening to her father's favorite Neil Diamond and Barbara Streisand recordings. The music, which had played in her childhood home almost every day, had brought Richard Cole back to her in ways standing among his possessions couldn't. She had cried so much during the ride north that the exhaustion in her back couldn't compare to the weariness in her soul. After allowing herself to feel such tremendous agony, it surprised Kristen how her well of grief was still so near to the surface.

"I'm so very sorry for your loss," said Tony in a heavy voice, his dark eyebrows furrowed, revealing the first lines of wisdom that would one day etch into his brow. "He was a good man and very kind to me."

After a moment passed, Tony stepped back.

"Well, I'd better go then," he told her. "My condolences, again, for your loss."

"What did he want you to work on?" Kristen asked as he turned to leave.

Tony paused, shaking his head as if it didn't matter.

"Your father was looking to renovate the house. We had discussed giving me a chance to do the work slowly. I'm just starting out in this business, so I don't have many references. I offered to do the work for free if he'd let me photograph the finished work for my portfolio."

Tony stopped and looked up at the house behind Kristen.

"She's so beautiful. And Richard didn't have the money to restore her, not like she deserves. When I finished, I thought she'd make the best resume I could ever hope for."

"Ah," Kristen sighed empathetically. "I wish I could let you do that, but the house has an equity mortgage, and I can't afford it. I'll be dipping into my little savings just to make payments until she sells."

"I understand," Tony nodded, his smile finding its way back, even if only a bit.

"My real estate agent is helping me find a design firm to handle a quick remodel to prepare it for sale. But I'd be happy to give your card to the next owner. Perhaps they might be interested in your offer to do a more complete restoration," Kristen offered. She shrugged and added, "You never know, right?"

The young man nodded after considering her offer.

"That's very good of you. I'd appreciate that," Tony answered, reaching into his back pocket to find his wallet. After a brief search, he extended his business card to Kristen, who received it and read his name aloud.

"Tony De Luca. I'm so glad you stopped by," she said, extending her hand to him.

He took her hand and thanked her one last time before returning down the long path to the street.

My god, she thought as she watched him turn onto the sidewalk and move away, *that's one beautiful man.*

CHAPTER FOUR

"HE KEPT MANY THINGS IN HIS OFFICE, BUT MUCH OF what's there is private," Chancellor Pomeroy admitted. "I could have it all boxed and brought over to you, but I'd like you to consider coming in yourself. For your own closure, Kristen. It'll give you another chance to grieve properly. Your photo is everywhere in that small room. You should see how he made sure your smile was with him throughout his day."

Kristen could think of little she wanted to do less, though she knew the man was right. Another chance to grieve would make saying goodbye easier.

"I'm not sure I can," said Kristen. "Will you let me think about it for a while?"

"Of course, dear," the older man said warmly. "You have my number. I'll wait to hear from you."

Kristen thanked Pomeroy for his kindness. It seemed she had thanked dozens of people today. Her father's wake and funeral services had been simple, but the people who attended were warm and kind, as her father had always been. Several had offered to come early and help her prepare his house for the reception. Now surrounded by them all, she couldn't have been more grateful for their help.

Since he died, it felt like her strength had all but left her. They had also helped Kristen with her parent's bedroom. Richard's best friend had even gone into the bathroom and ensured no signs of the accident were left.

What was the value of that kindness? Kristen couldn't think about it too long without falling apart.

When they'd all said their last farewells, Kirsten fell into bed with complete exhaustion, offering her little choice but to fall asleep. Even thoughts of what she'd face the following day couldn't stop her mind from shutting down.

The donation trucks arrived first thing in the morning. Every bit of furniture would go, save her parents' bedroom set. The thought of having to sleep in that room filled Kristen with more than a little anxiety, but she wouldn't let herself give in to irrational fear. Her mother's bedroom set of heavy polished oak, inlaid with handsome iron mouldings, was the finest piece of furniture in the dwelling and would look excellent during an open house. The realtor would stage the rest of the home when the renovations were complete.

The other factor in choosing to move into the main bedroom was its size and the need for enough space to hold her parent's private belongings. Photographs, books, their computers, her father's clinical studies; these things were everywhere in the house. One by one, she moved each item into the main bedroom and stored them in loosely organized piles. Kristen would examine everything this week and box up what she wanted to ship home to San Diego. The makeshift repository meant the house would otherwise be empty, and work could begin on the renovations without impediment tomorrow.

Kristen had been astonished to find daily journals her

mother had kept during her cancer treatments. Kristen never knew the woman had written such a chronicle; her father never mentioned it after Margaret's funeral. The thought of one day reading them was more than Kristen could think about now.

She had declined the design firm's offer to provide formal plans; no computer-generated rendering was necessary. Kristen was confident the company knew what they were doing, could execute it on budget, and finish quickly. Two and a half bathrooms, a new kitchen, and the house painted. The main bath had been the last bit of remodeling undergone before her parents had purchased the home, and they could leave it as-is, still in excellent shape. They would end with a modest upgrade of the yards, but that was it.

Kristen expected to be done and gone within the week; everything settled and left in her project manager's hands.

"This is Doctor Cole," she said, answering her phone later in the afternoon.

"Hello, this is Rob Fernandez."

"Oh, hello, Rob," said Kristen. "What's up?"

"I'm calling to let you know I won't be able to take the job," the man said in a sinking, low voice.

Kristen's heart stopped.

Fernandez had agreed to take on the role of site manager only days earlier. He was the only agreeable response after Kristen exhausted herself to call every option within thirty miles.

"I've been offered another project that will take me through next year, and it's not something I can afford to turn down," he said. "I wanted you to hear it from me as soon as possible."

"What do you mean?" Kristen's voice rose. "You're

supposed to be here in the morning. The contractors start the demolition work at eight o'clock."

"Yeah, I'm really sorry to do this to you, but there's no way around it for me."

Kristen felt a dozen graphic insults rush to her mouth, but she didn't have the strength to speak a single one. Instead, she quietly swiped to end the call.

You miserable little... Kristen's mind flooded with anger, but she wouldn't let herself cry. There was no time to ponder all the things she ought to tell the man... or the Better Business Bureau. Instead, Kristen adopted her game face, the shield she relied upon in every counseling session.

"Just fix it," she whispered.

She would start over that very moment. Kristen had a week to find a replacement. Until then, she'd be there every day to pretend she had any notion of what proper oversight entailed on a construction site.

Kristen found her way to the front porch, feeling the first break in the heat of summer draw her to sit on the steps. She opened the small leather wallet portfolio where she kept her iPhone and began a Google search. As Kristen typed 'Construction Project Manager Cambria' into the search field, her distracted grip on the large case caused one of the wallet's occupants to fall out of its sleeve and onto the step beneath her.

She reached to recover it and lifted the simple white business card.

'Tony De Luca,' it read.

Kristen only hesitated a moment before dialing the card's printed telephone number into her phone.

"Hello?" his deep voice answered her call.

"Hi, Tony. This is Kristen Cole," she said agreeably. "We

spoke the other day. I'm Richard Cole's daughter. Do you remember me? You visited the house to check on my father."

"Of course, hello."

"I haven't forgotten what we discussed about the house," said Kristen, "and though nothing's changed with my plans, I wondered if you might consider the site manager job I mentioned. The guy I had lined up just quit on me, and I need someone to step into the role as soon as possible."

As no answer came from the young man, Kristen continued.

"I realize you had other ideas for the house, but perhaps it would still be a step in the right direction for you? I plan on returning to San Diego at the end of the week, and I'll need someone to be here every day for the next six months to oversee the contractors my design firm has lined up."

Kristen felt her inner salesperson push through his continued silence.

"I don't expect there's much for you to add to the project, not like you talked about the other day. But who knows? You might find something extra you can bring to work during that time. I have twelve thousand dollars budgeted for the position and wanted to know if you're interested."

She had finished her spiel and left the ensuing silence in the young man's court.

"Hello?" she said, with unexpected impatience.

"Um, yeah," Tony answered in time. "That would be cool."

Kristen smirked and closed her eyes. She mouthed the word 'cool' in silent satisfaction.

THE SCALE OF THIS OPPORTUNITY WAS NOT LOST ON Tony—quite the opposite. He'd become anxious after speaking with Kristen Cole on the phone yesterday. Sleep didn't come fast once he reviewed his notes, the manifesto of his vision for the restoration, created after he'd approached her father with his offer.

Though Tony had agreed his role would be an on-site coordinator for another designer's remodel, the young man was adamant he'd exploit any chance to do more during the six months at hand. Everything extra Tony could do would be one more photograph he could take.

He arrived at seven-thirty that morning. The lack of sleep was a minor ache in his head, but he'd stopped at a coffee shop on the way into town, asking for a simple cup of black. But the sight of the house spiked his adrenaline more than the coffee ever could. Tony took a deep breath once he stood up from his truck, took in the silent sea air, and started the path toward the house with his notebook.

It took Kristen a while to greet him at the front door. She seemed surprised to find Tony on her porch.

"Hi, I didn't expect you for another hour," she said with a hint of impatience.

"Demo starts in half an hour?" Tony asked, looking at his wristwatch.

"They said eight o'clock," she answered with a similar impatience.

"That gives me twenty-seven minutes to review the site," he answered with confusion.

"Really?" Kristen turned to find the wall clock no longer hung on the now empty living room wall. "Damn it. I'm so sorry. Come in, please."

"That's cool," Tony smiled and stepped over the threshold, letting her close the front door behind him.

"Really, I am sorry. I'm not a morning person, not even slightly. Give me a few to finish up, and I'll be down for you in a few," she promised him, moving back to climb the stairs.

"Not at all—take your time. I'll have a look around the downstairs," Tony said, lifting his paper cup to take a sip of coffee.

He realized her hair was soaking wet and combed back in a hurry as if he'd run her out of the shower. Indeed, he thought. Not a morning personal at all.

The house was, of course, much larger now that it stood empty. The vacancy gave Tony his first proper look at what the handsome structure had to work with and what it didn't have. Her floors were a beautiful hardwood, but no one had polished them in decades, if ever. Worn pockets appeared in high-traffic spaces where earlier owners hadn't laid runners. The living room also had minor stains; unattended wine spills had seeped through a rug and discolored the hardwood. They couldn't be re-polished until he sanded the floors down and re-stain them.

As Tony moved through the rooms, he continued to see

36

areas that needed attention—the wainscoting in the dining room; the door in the powder room; bookshelves in the study by the second fireplace; the ceiling crown in the hallway. Tony also saw how unremarkable the downstairs bedroom was, with its characterless walls and a bathroom door that didn't match any other. He wouldn't let the job finish without adding something in here.

But the kitchen was a whole other matter. It was already smaller than what modern home shoppers wanted. But it took Tony by surprise that the previous owners had never taken the slightest interest in style or beauty. Richard Cole had joked about how it all seemed badly done when he gave Tony his first tour, but the room was an unqualified failure.

Each component was a mistake: the floor, the counters, the cabinets, the tile backsplash, the window frames, and even the ceiling. Someone had stood here and made a dozen terrible choices, each unfathomable to Tony. It's simple enough to change appliances, but the rest? Better to take the room down to its studs and start over.

Making his way back to the front of the house, Tony found a coat closet under the stairs and switched on the overhead lamp to examine the space. Homeowners seldom give much attention to closets, but this one was about as rough as they got. With a shake of his head, Tony examined the crudely sawn wood in disappointment. The single coat of off-white paint was so thin he could see the boards' natural discolorations through it. Overhead was a cheap metal fixture fastened to the ceiling. It bore a solitary lightbulb sticking out of its base at an awkward angle.

The boards had become warped at the back of the closet near the floor, a likely sign of water damage. To be sure, Tony walked into the closet and bent down to crouch where the space inverted under the staircase. There, he ran his hand on the bubbled panel. It was dry but cold to the touch. A light draft brushed past his skin from the uncovered floor seam, and he ran his finger there to see if he could pull the board up and out.

The lightbulb above his head shattered with a loud pop, giving Tony a startle that caused him to fall onto his side with a heavy thud. He shut his eyes against the small slivers of glass that landed around him. Tony shook out his dark brown hair to make sure he could open his eyes before standing up to move out of the closet.

From overhead, he heard Kristen's shoes move through the house and down the stairs. Tony stood up slowly, careful to wipe the glass off his jeans. Stepping with caution to avoid crushing the larger pieces of glass, he unbuttoned the front of his gray flannel shirt and peeled it off to shake out any glass that might still hang to the fabric.

"What happened?" Kristen said from behind him.

"Had my first accident, I'm afraid," Tony replied, attempting to keep his voice calm.

"Did you knock the bulb out?" she asked. Glass clinked onto the floor as he shook out his shirt.

"No, I was on the ground sizing up that board at the back. I thought we might have water damage. And then the lightbulb just exploded overhead."

When Tony was out of the closet, he brought the shirt around his shoulders and over his thin and sleeveless white undershirt. He looked up to find Kristen staring at his tattooed shoulders with a light scowl.

"No need to call the paramedics. I'll be just fine, thanks," he said in exasperated jest.

When Kristen didn't respond, Tony attempted a smile to lighten her expression. But nothing changed in her eyes until they shifted toward the front door. He turned to see two men standing on the front porch ringing the doorbell.

"Are you gonna sweep this?" Kristen asked, her voice still colored with mild impatience.

"Here." he said, reaching to shut the closet door. "Stay out of there for now, and I'll take care of it before I leave. Let's go introduce ourselves to the crew."

"Right," Kristen acknowledged, and she walked to answer the front door.

What the hell? he thought. It wasn't the first sour look Tony had weathered from people over his ink, the patterns etched over his shoulders and back in heavy shades of gray and black. But it ate at him each time it happened.

Tony shook it off and nodded to the demolition team as Kristen introduced him.

CHAPTER SIX

KRISTEN FELT SURE TONY NEVER MEANT TO BOTHER her. She knew he only ever wanted to do a good job. And regardless of all the reasons he'd given her to doubt his performance, Kristen would take an honest, engaged effort over error-free work any day. Tony had a powerful drive to create something great, and she admired him for it.

But now Kristen couldn't stop herself from watching him. And she wouldn't find that bit of compulsion so distracting if the guy would keep on his shirt.

The late summer heat flooding the house was oppressive by mid-day. And they couldn't use the air conditioner to offer relief because of the construction dust. He'd sealed the vents to keep debris out of them. The result was a demolition team of five men working in thin wife-beaters drenched with sweat. That would've distracted her enough, but then there was Tony.

In Kristen's work life, dressing in anything more revealing than business casual attire was a borderline criminal offense. She'd often suffered through dress code staff meetings just because someone showed up in a t-shirt or tight blue jeans.

Perhaps her rigid corporate background was the reason Kristen felt so unprepared to face the opening act of *Thunder Down Under* in her living room while they tore up the house. She made a conscious choice to hold her tongue and keep to her room whenever she could.

Kristen answered a knock on her bedroom door, opening it to find Tony standing there without even his undershirt.

"What's up?" she managed, paralyzed by his calendar pin-up physique and confused by his intense gaze.

Without a word, Tony entered her room and closed the door behind him.

The act baffled Kristen. The familiarity implied by Tony's silence, his deep expression, and the impertinence of his behavior left her speechless.

Tony turned his back on her and crossed the room to the windows overlooking the rear yard.

My god, he's going to make me look at his tattoos again, she thought to herself.

It was not simple for Kristen to be ignored in this manner, certainly not in her own home. But she couldn't utter any of the hundred choice phrases that swirled impatiently in her mind. Instead, she resigned herself to stay silent and observe him.

The tattoos. They distracted Kristen even more than his hard shoulders ever could. How to explain what it was about tattoos on a man's body? She didn't have any great love of them—frankly, Kristen had never seen a tattoo that warranted any genuine admiration for the artistry behind its design. However, on a man's body, their effect on Kristen was highly erotic— palpable, even. She couldn't help but become aroused. Perhaps the root of her attraction was how the canvas of a man's body moved underneath the art. It was wise for Kristen to wait for Tony to speak—she couldn't have composed an intelligent sentence if she'd tried.

"I've been waiting for you," he said to her. "I've been without comfort for more than a year now."

Kristen couldn't fathom what Tony meant. She moved closer to him to ask for his meaning but found herself unable to take her eyes off his body; the sculpture of his broad back, the precision of the musculature in the intense mid-day light that flooded past him. The imagery on his shoulder was the most distracting part—the *Vitruvian Man*. DaVinci's nude male traveled down to the dents of his upper arms, and the sight suddenly more than Kristen could stand.

"Will you let me love you?" he asked.

Kristen's breathing became erratic. It was all she could do to keep her eyes open. She touched Tony's shoulder, sliding her hand over his arm's soft hardness. Kristen felt as if she wanted to lay her head against him.

He turned around to face her.

Standing before Kristen were the eyes of another man. Steel-blue irises under a dark brow that implored her with desire.

"Touch me again," he said, pulling her hands to his hard chest.

Kristen jolted in bed to the sound of loud knocking. Her eyes opened to see the early morning light blazing into her bedroom.

Again, the knocking came. *The front door downstairs*, she thought, *they're here already.*

Kristen moved her limbs, still made of iron, as quickly as she could. She had gone to bed in an oversized Lady Gaga concert t-shirt and an old pair of high-cut gym shorts. Kristen thought nothing of making her way downstairs wearing them. The woman was more concerned about running her hands through her hair in a futile attempt to tame the flaming red curls. They had escaped Kristen's scrunchy as she slept, a fate that befell them most nights.

"Sorry, good morning," she said to Tony, her eyes squinting at the day's light they hadn't adjusted to yet.

"Good morning," he answered. He seemed to hold back a grin reading her black t-shirt's three giant pink words: 'LADY FUCKING GAGA.'

"I'm going to have a key copied for you today," promised Kristen.

"No worries," Tony answered. "I brought you a coffee."

He laid the beverages on the dining room sideboard. The built-in had become the only proper surface left to them, short of the floor, now that the kitchen no longer existed.

The heavy scent of the coffee made its way to Kristen's brain well before she became conscious of his offer.

"That's sweet of you. Thanks a lot," she smiled. Kristen found all four packets of sugar and, lifting the lip, dropped them into her cup.

"Sweet tooth," said Tony, his eyebrows raised. "Well, don't worry. I take it black."

"I remember," she winked.

The surrounding house had become a war zone, or so Kristen thought. The bathrooms and kitchen were empty shells, their contents destroyed and cleared out yesterday.

"You said we're doing the ceilings today?"

"I'll work on the ceilings if possible," Tony confirmed. "But I aim to get a plumber and electrician here to examine what we have. We need to determine if a larger replacement of the piping or wiring is necessary before we reinstall the drywall. Hopefully, they won't need to do anything too difficult."

Kristen stared at anything but Tony's eyes as he spoke.

"You okay?" he asked.

The coffee kicked in all at once, and Kristen became irritated by her behavior. *What the hell is wrong with me?* If a guy ever did such a thing to her, Kristen's inner feminist warrior would be hard-pressed to hold back the venom of her response. But whenever she was around the kid, she couldn't think straight. And now, possibly the most humiliating part, she was dreaming about the fucker!

"Listen, I need to apologize to you for yesterday," she started. "I could say I'm grieving over my loss and that I'm not in my right mind, but that doesn't excuse how I was short with you."

From his expression, it was clear Tony hadn't expected such an omission or apology.

"I don't want you to think I don't appreciate your being here. Frankly, you're a lifesaver for showing up with less than a day's notice. And I appreciate how you jumped into this all without a sure footing. So, thank you. I apologize for how quickly I raised my voice over every little thing yesterday. You're learning to do your role, but that's no excuse for my behavior. After you went home for the day, it mortified me to realize how disrespectful I'd been to you, especially in front of the contractors."

Tony shook his head as if he didn't need to hear anymore.

"It's fine, really," he assured her. "I wasn't crazy about your delivery, I'll admit, but I agreed with most of what you said. So, apology accepted."

"Great," she said, taking a second sip. "Also, if you ever want to get on my good side, coffee is the way to go."

Kristen lifted her cup in a salute of cheers and shot him a proper smile.

"I'm not an amateur at everything," he smirked.

"Good. Now one last thing," said Kristen.

Tony's eyes widened with comic timing.

"I know it was warm in here yesterday, and today will bring more of the same." Kristen paused, looked away to collect herself, and then returned with a heavy breath. "I need you guys to keep your shirts on for me. To be honest, that had a lot to do with why I was so difficult. I was already feeling out-of-sorts with all the noise and destruction, and then finding you guys posing for a muscle calendar... became a problem for me."

Tony squinted as if worried by her statement and started to respond before Kristen cut him off.

"I'm not trying to read you a list of OSHA violations," she said. "Seriously, it's not that big a deal. But I just don't feel comfortable here alone with a bunch of almost topless men. How about some T-shirts instead of tank tops? Is that a reasonable compromise?"

"Like that one?" Tony nodded at the expletive on her chest.

Kristen looked down to realize what she wore and laughed, drawing her hands up to her eyes.

"Again, I'm the problem here. I fully admit to that," she answered. "What do you want me to say? I'm an indoor cat, as you likely noticed, and well out of my comfort zone. I'm just asking for something that covers up a bit more.

"No, that's fine," Tony conceded. "I understand what you mean. I'll make sure it happens."

"Thank you," she shook her head. "And for real, after I'm gone on Sunday, you guys can have whatever dress code you want. Nude construction island if it helps you work better. Deal?"

"Fair enough," he nodded in agreement.

"Besides getting that key made for you, I'm going out to

visit my father's office at CalPoly today. They've asked me to collect his belongings. I don't know how long it'll take, but I'll have my cell phone on if you need me."

"Very good. I'll start my day," Tony answered, heading to the kitchen.

CHAPTER SEVEN

KRISTEN MET CHANCELLOR POMEROY AT THE FACULTY office building after struggling to find the correct spot for nearly half an hour. Her father had never brought her to the campus before, and California Polytechnic State University, called CalPoly by students and professors, was anything but small and intuitively laid out. Moreover, the faculty buildings were rather unimpressive compared to the massive and arresting structures that housed its many classrooms.

"Welcome, Kristen!" the jolly man said to her, pocketing the cell phone he'd used to give her turn-by-turn instructions during her walk from the faculty parking lot.

"Thank you so much for your help, Chancellor," she said, extending her hand to him.

"Please, call me Patrick," he said.

"Thank you, Patrick," Kristen smiled. "This is some campus, all right. My father once told me how early he would need to arrive to avoid being late for his lectures, and I see why now. Driving through it all was no small order."

"It certainly keeps me fit," laughed Patrick, patting the bulging midsection underneath his white button-down dress shirt and navy necktie. "Come on in. I want to introduce you to the department chair."

He led Kristen through the building past a half dozen similar offices, where many students waited in the hallways to meet with their professors. In time, the two arrived at a closed door with a title plaque that read 'Valerie Jameson, Psychology Department Chair,' and Patrick knocked before entering.

"Doctor Jameson?" he asked, peering his head inside the room.

"Yes, come in," she said, standing up when Kristen followed the chancellor inside the small office.

Jameson was a heavy-set blonde in her early fifties who smiled behind a large pair of severe black-framed glasses.

"Doctor Jameson, this is Doctor Kristen Cole, Richard's daughter," he said in a low, confidential voice.

"Oh, welcome, Doctor Cole. It's very good to meet you at last. I'm so sorry I wasn't able to attend your father's services. Won't you please come in," Jameson said, gesturing to the open chairs in front of her desk.

"It's a pleasure to meet you," said Kristen, taking a seat.

"I'm going to leave you here for now, Kristen. Doctor Jameson can show you to your father's office," Pomeroy assured her. "Will you call me before you leave?"

"Of course, thank you for your help," Kristen promised, before the chancellor returned to the hallway and closed the office door behind him.

"We were all so upset by your father's passing," Jameson said. "Despite how many of us there are, we rely on one another to run the university. So, we develop friendships fast. Richard was precious to my colleagues and me. I'm sure you gathered that by how many of us were at the services."

"I'll admit I was surprised," Kristen answered. "A very

moving surprise. It was so touching that the Chancellor himself came. I didn't expect that."

"I'm glad you noticed because your father meant a lot to them," said the woman. "He was such a special man. Richard was a mentor to many of the faculty here who are still on the tenure track. The light in his eyes was infectious when he taught his classes. His student ratings were some of the highest we've ever had at the school. And Richard's sense of humor..."

Kristen felt the emotion gathering behind her eyes, and they scouted about the room to find the tissue she would need in a minute.

"Well, let me take you to his office," Jameson said, rising again to move across her office, where she held open the door for her guest.

The woman led Kristen to a different hallway of offices, soon arriving at one with her father's name still printed on the door plaque. She inserted a key to unlock it and turned the handle.

"I've told no one you're here, so you can do this in peace. I don't want you to be disturbed, and I presume you don't want to see anyone. There are boxes in the corner for you to use. Just let me know if you need more. Whatever you don't want to take—the files and such—I'll have them shredded and recycled for you," Jameson offered.

Upon sight of the room, an overwhelming pain struck Kristen. Crossing the threshold, she saw her face staring back at her from several photographs in frames atop the credenza behind his desk.

"Thank you, I appreciate it," Kristen managed to say before falling silent.

"Just call me for anything. My office line is programmed

on that first speed-dial button," she said, pointing to the black plastic telephone on his desk.

When the office door shut, Kristen's frame became unbalanced with heavy sobs of crushing grief. She had to place her hand on the wall to hold herself upright. It was just as the chancellor had described it, this room. Dad had installed something almost everywhere to remind himself of his only child.

Besides the dozens of photographs of his wife and daughter, Richard Cole had brought an overwhelming number of knickknacks to his office to remind himself of their lives. On the credenza were handprints in white plaster with the words 'For Daddy, Happy Father's Day' scrawled in blue paint in a child's sloppy handwriting. A clay ashtray stating the same message sat on the desk. Kristen's acceptance letter from the University of California at San Diego hung framed on the wall, something she never realized her father had taken. Beside it was a framed high school report card from Kristen's junior class year and the letter informing his daughter of her SAT scores. Also on the wall was a small frame containing Kristen's business card from the research hospital where she worked.

She hadn't been prepared to find these things here. It made little sense to Kristen how her father had brought so many items to sit in an office where he spent only a few hours each week.

Despite the outpouring of loving memories surrounding her, Kristen's mind drifted to a hard time, the argument she and her father had one night over her mother.

"You're not to speak to your mother that way," he had said to her when she was fifteen. "Do you understand me?"

"Why are you taking her side?" Kristen railed. "You know

how she is. I can't take her bullshit anymore. I won't, Daddy! I don't want to live in the same house with her."

"And you're not to use that language with me, either," Richard answered firmly.

His last command had infuriated her. Kristen had relied on her father to be the referee between her and her mother for years. The woman seemed to find the way to Kristen's underbelly every time. The very sound of her mother's voice pushed the girl's buttons. And to hear her father patronize her now about her language was tantamount to betrayal. What difference did her language make? She hated the dumb cow, and to Hell with her!

"I expect you to respect us both, and you'll never again say what you said to her tonight. I won't stand for it."

"What about what she said to me?" the girl howled, her voice breaking.

Her father's opinion meant everything to Kristen. The emotions of frustration and anger swept the girl off her bearings when he ordered her to stop. It was bad enough she'd told her mother to fuck off and drop dead, but now to see the disappointed expression in her father's eyes was even more painful than the row had been.

Richard seemed to wait for Kristen to calm herself. Before she'd realized it, he was sitting beside her on the bed in her room, where they'd imprison her for the rest of the summer. He placed his arm around her in time, bringing tears down over her flushed cheeks. She buried her head in his chest.

"What she said to you didn't give you license to act as you did," the man said, his tone grave. "Nothing she'll ever say to you could make your words tonight acceptable. I know she hurt you, but your next move should have been to come to me and let me handle it for you, not say the mindless things you did."

The girl only wept in response.

"Do you understand, Krissy? She's your mother, and this is her house. You will not disrespect her here ever again."

The girl continued to cry, her father's voice shaming her now just as much as his unfairness infuriated her.

"Promise me," he whispered.

And with those simple words, she gave in to her sorrow and nodded against his chest, shuddering in anguish.

He hugged Kristen and lifted her chin to kiss her cheek.

Kristen still felt the memory of her father's forgiving kiss fifteen years later. The shame of her behavior and tenderness of his love were more painful now without him than they'd ever felt when she was a girl.

There was a knock at the office door, and it opened.

"Hello?"

Kristen didn't answer but saw the face of a man with brilliant blond hair as he stood in the doorframe. He appeared to be the same age as Kristen, dressed in a blue button-down shirt with the collar open, his sleeves rolled to his upper arms. The man wore his shirt tucked into well-cut heather silk slacks with a deep brown belt clasped in burned silver. His feet wore shoes of brown patent leather crafted to appear worn but which surely came from some high-end designer's shop.

"Oh, I'm sorry," he said when he saw Kristen's pained face. "I saw Richard's light on, so I wondered who would be here. He was a friend of mine. You and I met the other day— you probably don't remember. At Richard's services?"

Kristen shook her head and attempted a polite smile, but it fell apart in less than a second. She brought her hands up to her face to shield her eyes from him, falling back to her sobbing.

After some time, she felt the man's arms enfold her, and

Kristen gave way to the stranger, burying her head in his chest. Kristen couldn't have said how long she cried, but she let the man hold her for some time before she could stop.

When she released enough of the pain and could collect herself again, the man guided Kristen to one of the guest chairs before her father's desk.

"The perfect room for a good cry, I imagine," he said warmly, sitting beside her. "I'm sorry I intruded."

"No, thank you. I can't tell you how badly I needed a hug," Kristen said, at last able to manage a small smile. "I remember your face, but the name is long gone. Forgive me."

"Not at all," he smiled back at her. "My name is Ryan. Your father was hands-down my favorite person in this whole place. I had lunch with him three times a week during the past year. He was the coolest guy I ever met."

"That's very sweet of you to say," Kristen offered. "I just got here and fell to pieces when I saw all this stuff. Chancellor Pomeroy told me I needed to come and see it for myself, but I didn't understand what he meant."

"I'll bet," said Ryan, his light blue eyes touring the space.

"It looks like he was building a shrine," Kristen sighed. "I worked with a lady whose cubicle was decked out like this at my first job. We all thought she was a weirdo."

He laughed at Kristen, flashing his movie star grin for a moment.

"I mentioned the same thing to Richard just after meeting him," Ryan confided. "I called him crazy, that is. He told me it was tough for him to return to work after retirement. So, he brought these treasures that reminded him of all his greatest achievements. The things that made him most happy and proud of a life well-spent. And, as everyone saw, the things in this room are almost all about you. He doesn't even have his diplomas on his office walls like the rest of us do. There's no space left for them, really."

Kristen felt it all overtaking her again.

"Before he told me that story, my office was as empty as I could make it," Ryan continued. "I didn't want any private items with me here. This place is about work, so I kept it separate from my private life. Your father changed my mind that day."

Ryan ran his hand along the base of his friend's Father's Day gift.

"I have nothing resembling this type of ...shrine, as you put it, but I've since brought in a few photographs of my friends and family to watch over me."

He smiled again, his eyes lighting up behind his tempered expression.

"Anyhow, they've fooled my students into believing I'm not such a cold duck."

Kristen laughed, taken with the man's humor and warm manner.

"Thank you for telling me that story," she said in time, a light smile taking her eyes. "I sure needed to hear it."

CHAPTER EIGHT

KRISTEN RETURNED TO THE HOUSE AROUND ONE-thirty in the afternoon with four boxes. She'd filled them with almost everything in her father's office.

The experience of sitting in his desk chair had been more fulfilling than Kristen ever dreamed. In the end, being in her father's private space had not only released her from the agony of the past days, it had left her with an unexpected sensation of contentment. Kristen would never say her father didn't want more time on this earth; he planned for years to manifest his dreams for retirement. But Kristen understood now that her father had lived such a full and joyful life, only her most selfish impulses could outweigh her feeling of contentment for him. This understanding and the resulting release had done more for her soul than all the tears ever could.

Ryan Hoffman had held Kristen as she walked through the wall of anguish. He'd shown her the truth that stood all around her, assisting her to see the beauty her pain was masking. For a psychologist to extend such praise toward a layperson was no small admission from a woman whose job was understanding the mechanics of the mind.

Ryan had asked to treat Kristen to a coffee tomorrow, which she had agreed to without a second thought. When she was driving away in her car, Kristen laughed at how quickly she'd agreed to his offer. Then again, if a serial killer offered her a latte, she might still have to think through the reasons she should decline.

It had been years since Kristen had met someone who had pressed all of her buttons the way Ryan had. It wasn't just that he was handsome—Kristen grew up in Southern California, where she passed a dozen cute guys jogging down the street or lifting in the gym every day. His financial accomplishment was another unremarkable feature in her world. It was that Ryan was awake. Kristen had seldom encountered a man so refreshingly intuitive and aware of the people around him.

Of course, she couldn't turn off her inner doctor, who analyzed her every emotion to exhaustion. Yes, Ryan was almost a carbon copy of her father. He was clever, insightful, gentle, attentive, and warm. Kristen had been through enough guys to know those features didn't grow on trees. Finding more than one of them in a man was enough to try them out in bed. But to come across an evolved mind that didn't exist within a toad of a body? It was as if a unicorn had walked up to her and smiled.

Kristen sighed to herself as the inescapable realization stifled her infatuation.

"He must have a tiny penis," the woman said aloud. "You can't have money, be unmarried, handsome, smart—and have a great dick. That's not how the universe works."

Unicorns aren't real, she understood.

"Unless they're gay, so gay," Kristen sang in tune with

Madonna as she turned up the volume to blare the track through her car's stereo.

She pulled up to her parent's home and carried her boxes up to the house. Once through the front door, she piled them on the foyer floor and called out to Tony to announce she was home. When he didn't respond, she found a small sheet of paper taped to the wall.

KRISTEN,

BOTH THE ELECTRICIAN AND PLUMBER CALLED IN TO CANCEL. ONE WILL BE OVER IN THE MORNING—THE OTHER MUST GET BACK TO ME. I'VE GONE TO MY WORKSHOP TO PREPARE PIECES TO REPLACE THE DINING ROOM CROWN. I'LL BE BACK IN THE MORNING.

TONY

All the peaceful calm Kristen had felt on her ride home fell away, replaced by a seething agitation.

"What the hell do you mean you've gone?" she said to the scrap of paper.

Kristen felt betrayed. She had accepted Tony's promise to be on-site five days a week, at least. On the weekends also, if necessary. He would work in the house and manage the job, not take the damned afternoon off on his second day without asking permission. And to think she'd apologized to him this morning. Commenting on his lassie-fair attitude was on the mark, she realized now.

Kristen looked in her phone to find his number, already shaking her head as if she couldn't wait for him to answer her call. But the woman stopped, convinced a simple phone call wasn't enough. She fumbled through the wallet case holding her phone and found Tony's business card.

1137 Los Olivos Avenue

There you are, she thought, adding the location to her phone book so the device's navigator, Siri, could guide her to Tony's shop. Grabbing her purse, Kristen made her way back to her car and brought up the map for guidance on the vehicle's screen.

After driving for some time, Kristen learned Tony lived a respectful distance from her parent's house in Los Ojos, three full hamlets down the coast. It resembled most other small towns that hugged the Pacific, though much of the area fell into a more modest market than Cambria. Of course, in California, that meant next to nothing. If you could see the ocean, a studio bungalow would still run you a half-million dollars.

The map guidance soon led Kristen to a cluster of warehouses with unmarked units. Undeterred, she parked her car in one of the few open spots along the street. After studying her phone, she gathered that Tony's business was on the backside of a smaller row of faceless buildings. Kristen guessed the best approach and stomped in that direction.

After soon coming to a dead-end, she spotted his beat-up blue pickup truck parked around the bend. Not twenty feet away was an open roll-up garage door with classic R&B music competing against the sound of a saw at work. Moving toward the spot, Kristen kept out of sight behind a white van parked near the door to avoid drawing the occupant's notice.

Perhaps this isn't the right unit, she thought.

Kristen verified the source of the noise was Tony. With his back to the open door, he stood over an infernal contraption through which he pushed long wooden boards, one after another. Tony wore a pair of large acrylic safety glasses and fluorescent orange colored earplugs. And, of course, he was topless—his white undershirt hung from the back of his cargo shorts.

All the urgency that had driven Kristen here faltered. Yes, he had left the site, but he was still working. In her mindless paranoia, Kristen realized she had expected him to be off playing at the beach or taking a siesta—anything but what she was paying him to do. The more she stared at him, the sweat covering his torso from the heat of the afternoon, the more Kristen felt like a fool.

It's me, she cringed with embarrassment. *It's always me, isn't it?*

Kristen would bring this up when she attended her monthly analyst appointment. Part of working as a clinical psychologist was attending frequent sessions with another psychologist. It's deemed crucial by the industry that a counselor has their mind analyzed often to ensure normal human problems don't become something that might interfere with their ability to treat their own patients. Kristen would arrive at her next session with a list of bullet points, the first of which would cover how unforgivably bad a manager of humans she was. It seemed she could fix the worst of their emotional problems but couldn't manage an employee to save her life.

Kristen backed up to walk away but stumbled as she bumped against the white van. She noticed the side doors were swung open, revealing a slick interior decked out with a custom living design. The vehicle was more of a small bus than a standard van. It appeared to be one of those tiny homes featured on HGTV—the ones people lived in as they drove from place to place on vacation.

There was a polished wooden counter with a sink and a small built-in oven. Against the far side was a handsome, darkly stained wooden sofa with charcoal cushions that appeared to transform into a full-sized bed. The walls bore bookshelves with metal-rimmed glass doors crafted to fit into the curving walls of the bus. Peering her head in, Kristen found a flat-screen display on the wall facing the sofa.

The music from Tony's workshop became clearer, though Kristen was too distracted to notice the saw being shut down. She turned around to find Tony staring at her from about thirty feet away, reaching to pull the orange plugs from his ears.

Adrenaline spiked through Kristen's system. It was all she could do to smile as if he hadn't surprised her.

"Hi!" Kristen spoke a bit too eagerly.

Tony pulled his shirt from his waist and drew it over his head.

"I wasn't expecting you to come down here," he answered with plain confusion.

"Oh, I'm sorry I didn't call, but I thought I would just drop in to see how you were getting on," Kristen said, feeling the thread of her response unraveling.

From somewhere she couldn't explain, a neuron fired in her spinning head, and she jerked to reach into her purse. After digging, she found a small paper bag and pulled it out.

"I stopped at Home Depot to get your key made this morning, and I wanted to make sure you had it ...so I'm not holding you up in the morning," Kristen said, handing him the little paper bag.

Tony's eyes closed, and he tilted his head as if he were upset.

"Oh, man. I'm so sorry, I forgot about the key. I was upset when they canceled on me, so I came back here to get some planer work done. I didn't want the afternoon to end up a total waste," he said, drawing his lips together in frustration.

"Oh, don't worry about it," Kristen said.

"No, really, I'm so embarrassed I caused you to come all the way down here," Tony pleaded.

"It's early, and it wasn't even thirty minutes away. Don't give it another thought," Kristen waved his comment away.

Tony shook his head, still frustrated with himself.

"So, give me a tour. Is this yours?" she asked, turning back to the bus.

"Yeah," he answered with boyish awkwardness. "She's all mine."

"Do you take her on trips?" Kristen continued.

"I sure do. But I keep her here."

"Oh? I expected you'd keep her at your home. Is it better for you to park it here at your business?"

"Well, yes, it's a lot easier," he tilted his head. "But that's because she is my home."

Kristen didn't understand him at first, but the simple fact soon clicked in her mind.

"Oh, you live on the bus?" she stared at it, her confusion clearing.

"Not for you?" Tony smiled. "I get that a lot."

"No," she shook her head, "it's just ...how do you do that? How do you get all your stuff in here? Half my clothes wouldn't fit."

"Well, to start, I don't have a lot of stuff," he smirked. "I did while living at home, but then I went through four apartments in four years. Have you ever moved that often? You learn fast what's important to you and what isn't."

"Still," Kristen said in disbelief, "you've got to have things. Can I see it?"

"Sure," he offered, stepping up into the van and reaching back for Kristen's hand to help her.

Climbing in, she realized they could both stand in the van without hunching.

Tony reached to pull out storage drawers under the sofa, beside the sink, and above the shelves, highlighting how his belongings hid everywhere in plain sight. Within each space, he'd organized the items with unique precision. Even his socks, of which he had dozens, aligned well enough that they looked like an IKEA display.

"It's a Marie Kondo fantasia," Kristen giggled.

"Who's that?" Tony asked.

"She's an organization goddess on Netflix. You should check her out," said Kristen. "But what about... I don't know... books?"

"I've got a few important ones there on the shelf," he nodded toward a small collection of hardcovers. "The rest are in my e-reader."

"Ah, I see," she said.

"You don't have your books on your pad?" he asked with another smirk.

"I'm an old lady, Tony. We used paper in my century."

"You're what ...five, six years older than me?" he squinted at her in mock disbelief.

"Yes, ...sure, I'll take it," she smirked. "I'm eight years older, and that was the cut-off point for paper book buyers."

"I see," said Tony.

"Oh, but that's what's missing. Where's the bathroom?" Kristen looked around at the space that seemed devoid of a toilet.

"Well, there's a half bath in my workshop," he nodded at the building. "And I take showers at the gym at least once daily."

Going there every day explains why you look like you do, she thought, stopping herself from blurting her opinion right out. Kristen couldn't help but smell Tony in these close quarters. It baffled her how certain men could sweat and smell even better than when they were clean.

"I'm afraid that's where I would have to bow out," Kristen admitted. "I couldn't live without my bathroom. I wasn't even comfortable sharing my bathroom with my ex-boyfriend."

"No?" asked Tony.

"I'm an only child," she smiled. "I never had to learn to share. In fact, my motto is, and I share this openly when I vacation with friends, that happiness is separate bathrooms."

Tony laughed and turned to step back onto the pavement, reaching his hand up to offer Kristen help.

"Then I can say without question this life isn't for you," he smiled as her feet returned to the asphalt.

Tony led Kristen into his workshop, pointing out the machines lining the walls. He described them to her as if they were precious to him.

Kristen couldn't help but feel affection for the guy. He was not her type, with his studio apartment on wheels and no bathroom, but Tony was about as sweet as he could be.

"I was using this one as you came in," Tony said, running his hand over the machine's surface to wipe off the remaining sawdust. "It's a planer, which I use to sand the boards down to get them straight and smooth."

"Well, I'm happy you had me drive all the way down here," she teased him. "This was an eye-opener, for sure."

"I'm really sorry about that," he said with a self-conscious timbre, his voice again frustrated.

"I'm not," she said. "I had a good time nosing my way through your life."

"I was glad to share it with you," Tony beamed. "I'm not an only child, so it was easy for me."

Kristen smiled at him and turned to make her way back through the driveway to the street.

"Thanks for being the smelly little brother I never wanted," she fired back. "I'll see you tomorrow morning."

"I'll try not to wake you up with all my stupid banging before you make it out of bed," he sneered.

"All the banging in the world couldn't get me out of bed before I'm done with it," said Kristen, unwilling to let him have the last word. She raised her hand to wave goodbye before recognizing the unintended double meaning of her comment.

CHAPTER NINE

Lily's Coffee House was a brightly colored bungalow set just off Main Street and crafted in a bohemian vibe. The exterior offered a small private garden with a covered patio bordered by vine-covered trellises to guard the shop's patrons against the minor noise from the street. The inviting space provided Cambrians with the perfect environment to sit, read, and relax. Even better, it offered breakfast all day, Kristen's favorite meal. She was a night owl and often running behind in the morning. It was a treat for her to enjoy more than a cup of coffee for breakfast.

Ryan had already seated himself at a little iron bistro table and stood up to greet her when their eyes locked. He dressed just as he did the day before, his professor's armor different only in its colors and textures. In the outdoor light, Ryan's hair glistened like polished gold.

"You look beautiful," he said, giving her a small kiss on the cheek.

The unexpected act gave Kristen a slight pause. She was unaccustomed to being greeted that way, even by close friends, but she smiled all the same.

"Thank you," said Kristen, and she took the seat he gestured towards in the shade.

"What would you like?" Ryan asked. "I need to order it for us inside, but they'll bring it out."

"I only had coffee in my mind, but the word 'breakfast' caught my eye as I walked in," Kristen said, scanning the small paper menu.

"I'm glad you said that," Ryan smiled. "I saw the same sign but didn't want to be the only one sitting at this table chowing away."

"Well, no need to worry," she said. "I'll have the breakfast bowl with bacon and a latte."

"Perfect," he replied and stood up to seek the counter inside the small bungalow.

Kristen couldn't help but watch Ryan as he walked away. She was always partial to a man who jumped up to serve a woman. She was also partial to a man with a nice backside.

The woman knew enough about herself to focus on perspective. When Kristen came across a man she liked, her unconscious tactic was to go all-in and fawn over the poor boy, a characteristic she loathed in herself. Worse for this one, she hadn't found a single thing about him that raised a red flag. Kristen would need to be responsible for herself now and observe Ryan with a critical eye.

When she was a girl, if a boy so much as looked in her direction, she planned the colors for their wedding. She supposed many young girls did the same thing—fantasized about what they'd tell their fairy godmother once cast in the role of Cinderella. But even now, in her early thirties, Kristen's imagination pondered that fantasy when she let her guard down.

For Kristen, it was a rather embarrassing secret she fought

to suppress. The worst thing about it was she didn't want to be married at this point in her life. Kristen thought marriage was a questionable decision for a woman, especially one with a career who wasn't ready for children. But the fifteen-year-old in her mind was still at work, scanning through catalogs to plan the cut of her future wedding gown.

Ryan returned with a plastic number affixed to a polished metal stand meant to mark their table for the service staff.

"The food should be out soon," he said. "There wasn't a line."

"Great," remarked Kristen as the lean man slid into his chair. "Listen, thank you again for yesterday. Last night, I imagined what that entire event must've been like for you. I don't know if I would've stopped everything for some wailing stranger, and been so kind and open—

"Of course you would," he interrupted her, drawing another smile from the woman's face.

"Eh, I'm not so sure," she winced. "But I want you to know how much it meant to me. So, thank you again."

"If I'm honest, I was jazzed just to get to speak with you," Ryan said. "I didn't expect to meet you again after the funeral, and I wanted to tell you how much I liked your father. He always lit up my day when we hung out."

Against her will, Kristen felt her eyes moisten.

"Shit, I'm sorry," she said. "There it goes again. Give me a second; I'll stop."

"No, wait, I'll stop," he said, shaking his head. "Let's talk about anything else. What books do you like? No, why am I asking you to talk more?"

Ryan shook his head. For the first time, she saw he was nervous.

"I'll talk," he continued. "I just finished reading a book

called Hegemony or Survival. It's by a political scientist who examines our country's foreign policy over the past eighty years."

"Oh, Christ," Kristen whispered. "By Chomsky?"

"You know it?" Ryan's eyes lit up with excitement.

"Yeah, the one who the dictators love? By any chance, did you get that book from my father?"

The man paused for a moment, recognizing what he'd done.

"Oh... yes. Richard recommended it to me. I'm sorry," he shook his head in embarrassment. "I can't believe I did that."

"That's okay. Keep going. If I cry again, don't worry. They'll be a different type of tears," Kristen smirked.

"So, you read it?"

"No, but he-who-shall-not-be-named went on and on about it at dinner once, so I'm familiar."

"Then I'll get right to my favorite part," he continued. "There was a section on the second Gulf War that discussed Chomsky's opinions for why the younger Bush's administration sought to remove the existing leadership in the region. Namely, to install a puppet regime in the way earlier administrations produced in North Africa and Central America."

Kristen nodded her head again and again as Ryan spoke. She had once applied for a counseling job that listed in great detail how a successful candidate must be able to nod their head up and down for several hours each day. She'd busted up over how someone bothered to write such a silly job requirement. But after ten years of doing just that, Kristen had to go out of her way to stop herself from nodding her head outside the office. She expected everyone presumed she was patronizing them. Frankly, she was always listening to people, and nodding was an involuntary reflex.

"They sent me to the middle east when I was a kid, so it stood out to me," he continued. "I turned eighteen a month after 9/11 and enlisted in the Navy the following day. Having faced our government's propaganda in that capacity, being so informed by that confined perspective, I've spent the rest of my life studying every other viewpoint of that period of our history. I study it to help me understand where we're heading as a nation and how it affects my business, but mainly as a hobby."

Kristen nodded again. It couldn't be helped.

"... I've also read *Harry Potter*," he smiled. "That was pretty wild, too."

Kristen laughed aloud at Ryan, at once grateful for the release.

"Well, thank god," she said. "I like a well-read guy."

I'm screwed, Kristen thought to herself. She was listening to a thirty-something replica of her father trapped behind a movie star's smile. Kristen began the count: Red-flag Number One.

A server arrived with their order on a tray. After a quick greeting, he placed each item on their table and asked if he could bring anything else. When they both declined, the server returned inside the cafe.

Kristen reached for her latte, finding the sugar dispenser at once.

"What's your business?" she asked. "You do something besides teaching, right?"

"Yes, I own a strategic defense consultancy. The business runs itself, and I retired from daily operations last year. Teaching was something I got into after taking a back seat to fill up my days, if I'm honest."

"Wow, you did *that* well with it?" Kristen asked, unable to hide her look of surprise.

"Very well," he said, adopting a confident posture. "When I got out of the Navy, I used the GI Bill for a ticket to Yale. While I was there, I met several students whose parents hail from some lofty perches. By the time I graduated, we were off and running with a clientele base that made things happen a lot faster than your normal lemonade stand might. Five years later, ...well, the last thing that would ever get me up in the morning is more money than I could need. You could say I'm looking for the next thing to dream about."

"And you hoped to find that teaching?" Kristen eyed him with suspicion.

"Absolutely!" he countered. "They have some of the brightest minds in computer science and aerospace engineering at CalPoly. And I'm learning more about both as I teach those foundations to fresh minds. You don't know where the great ideas will come from until they happen, but they won't happen just by telling disinterested folks with money how you'd do their job better."

"Fair enough," she said. "Well, I was feeling all accomplished about my career before I sat down, but it seems I went to the wrong school."

"What do you mean? UCSD is the top school in bio-molecular research."

"Well, sure, but I didn't get into *that* part of the university," Kristen laughed. "Those kids were building little fusion reactors with Legos when they were still in the crib."

"But you're happy with the work you do?" Ryan asked.

"Thrilled," said Kristen. "Every day is a puzzle to solve, and I need that sort of challenge to feel accomplished."

"Well, that's perfect," Ryan smiled. "That kind of happiness is all that matters at the end of the day. That's what I'm after."

Kristen loved the man's enthusiasm and his love for life. The smile that arrived on his face when he spoke about the things that motivated him was infectious.

"That and an exceptional woman to share my life with," Ryan added.

CHAPTER TEN

Getting ready for bed that night, Kristen felt euphoric. It was a sensation that often followed a great first date, but Ryan had pulled off something rather special that afternoon. He had excited her so much, Kristen considered what it might be like to move to Cambria. Anyone who knew Kristen understood she had zero desire to leave San Diego, much less for a sleepy town on the central coast of California. That had been her parent's dream, one based on peace and quiet, which resulted from an inherent lack of people.

If Kristen ever considered moving away, it would be for another metropolis—Los Angeles, San Francisco, or Seattle. It was in Kristen's self-interest, as it was for most Americans, to locate herself where many people lived together to increase her options for industry and livelihood. Cities didn't just happen because people prefer to live in cramped quarters that cost three-fold what they do in the quiet country. Cambria had the second disadvantage of falling on the California coastline, where homes still cost a fortune, even in lowly populated areas.

But Ryan was adamant it would be an excellent choice

for Kristen. There was plenty of work in California's middle for someone with her skills and experience. Ryan also touted the opportunities available for her to teach at the university. He promised they would take her in a heartbeat, considering the impact her father had made there. Ryan even noted that the great Bay Area cities were only a couple of hours away.

Ryan had grown up in Vallejo and expected he might end up in San Francisco or San Jose one day. These were not subtle hints he dropped. The man possessed a fiercely singular vision when he spoke of the future. It was a map laid out with perplexing precision, considering Ryan had admitted to his present search for the next emanation of his life.

For Kristen, there was something tantalizing about not closing that door with her normal knee-jerk response. She even kept open that place within her mind where only logic ruled—the central governance in charge of all critical decisions. Kristen wondered what being with a man like Ryan might be like. His bravado for her career implied he wouldn't mind if she worked, but would that change once they left the altar? Could Kristen fool herself into believing her satisfaction and happiness would last for more than a year as a housewife?

Walt Disney's rendition of *Cinderella* was about what happened to the lucky girl *before* she got married—the services she provided to her stepmother and step-sisters as their slave. It mentioned nothing about what happened to Cinderella the day after she took her vows.

Most of the "Housewives" on Bravo worked outside the home—being on that show itself was a job. Kristen hadn't gotten Ryan to say he wanted a family, but he never disputed the idea. Every man in his mid-thirties expects to field the question of marriage. The topic comes up even from much younger women. And what discussion of marriage could exclude the subject of children?

But those were topics for another day.

Once in bed, Kristen thumbed through her phone for only a few minutes, a personal best, before placing it on the charger and rolling over for the night. Her eyes were closed for a moment when a sharp noise from downstairs shot them open again. Kristen fumbled to turn on the bed's side-table lamp.

What happened then was nothing less than an internal argument about the very nature of fear. Entering the court, the Defense insisted there was no good reason for Kristen to be scared. After all, she was in a quiet neighborhood with a low crime rate. If her parents had ever installed a fan in this room, Kristen wouldn't have heard the noise. Back home, the white noise of her bedroom fan put her to sleep in about five minutes each night.

The Prosecution arrived in court with a dossier of every rape story a patient ever shared with Kristen. It also brought along a copy of every horror film she'd ever seen in her life. The Prosecution then played an edited cut of those films featuring a woman alone in a house out in the creepy woods who soon met her fate in some grisly manner. Most legal experts would agree the Prosecution gave the Defense a solid run for its money.

Kristen got out of bed, popped her shoes on, and walked to her bedroom door. She took along her cell phone, of course. Most of those victims would've made it to the end of the movie just fine had they remembered to bring their cell phones to call the police while fleeing down the street. Hell, the damned thing weighed so much, she could kill an intruder just by chucking the phone right at him.

Before setting foot in the hallway, Kristen flipped the light switch to illuminate her path. She did this to each switch she came upon during her short but unpleasant journey.

Let's light this bad boy up, shall we?

Arriving downstairs amid a symphony of boards creaking under each step, Kristen didn't need to look far to find the source of the disturbance.

A bucket of... was it plaster? The bucket had fallen off the edge of the sawhorse table. The white dust inside had fallen out when the cover had popped off during the crash. Kristen had no intention of cleaning it up for Tony. It would take all her focus to calm down and sleep tonight after her terrifying death walk. In the morning, Tony would no doubt have it swept up before Kristen opened her eyes.

As she started back to the stairs, Kristen noticed the home's security system keypad affixed beside the front door. Its LED display noted the system was ready for arming, a statement that signified all the doors and windows were closed. When she arrived in Cambria, Kristen had considered arming the system, but the idea didn't survive once she found a soft bed. She was only vaguely aware of how it worked. But still feeling the chills after her midnight venture downstairs, Kristen became more self-confident in examining her options.

She pulled open the keypad cover and found basic directions for using the device. Kristen could guess the code: her mother's birthday. Dad had used that code in the house when she was a child, and it had never changed while her parents lived in San Diego.

Punching in the sequence, the device posted the word 'Error' on the display and delivered an abrupt beep to signify Kristen's failure. After a second attempt, she surrendered to the obvious and proceeded back upstairs. It took more than a little self-discipline to turn the lights off as Kristen walked down the path to her bedroom. In the end, the upstairs hall remained lit when she closed her bedroom door, a reasonable compromise between lawyers for the Prosecution and Defense.

Kristen laid down again, taking a moment to find a cheap floor fan in her Amazon app to purchase for delivery the day after the next. She might only use it a few nights before returning home, but those nights promised far better sleep.

Of course, Kristen's laser-primed hearing picked up every minor sound in the room and house. As the building settled, she remembered the powder downstairs, dusted out by gravity over an area three feet from the unsealed bucket. The Prosecution offered one last-ditch effort, though the case was settled. Kristen recalled a scene in the film *Paranormal Activity* when the harassed couple scattered flour all over the upper floor of their home to get evidence of a malevolent presence. The protagonist's camera then caught footage of the three-toed demon walking through the hallway at night to their bedroom, only to stop and stand beside their bed.

Kristen didn't do well with the idea of demon possession, a fact that amused her as much as it annoyed her. Kristen worked in a profession devoted to the idea that demons were only the products of imagination. People who studied religion, either deeply or haphazardly, believed that demons existed in the spiritual world, even if they never saw one or knew someone who had. Psychologists and psychiatrists understood that what people considered demon possession was, in fact, a traumatic mental illness manifesting itself in a patient's behavior. The terrifying words or actions doctors confronted were the sad result of many forms of schizophrenia or Dissociative Identity Disorder.

However, when Kristen was about nine years old, her best friend's father allowed her to watch the film adaptation of

Peter Blatty's novel, *The Exorcist*. In the man's defense, which she didn't think he deserved, he'd told Kristen and Andrea to take their game of hide-and-seek outside. This was not a movie they should watch. Of course, what better marketing tool existed than to tell children they couldn't do something interesting?

After the girls continued to peek in and watch parts of the movie, Andrea's father gave up his protestations, and they ended up on the sofa beside him. It might have been because Andrea's father was very Catholic, proudly touting more than a dozen books about the Jesuits on his bookshelves. But he soon answered their questions regarding the terrifying girl in the movie. More to the point, he responded to their questions as if he were narrating a documentary. As a result, Kristen slept in her parent's bed for months afterward, resulting in a heated argument between the two fathers.

Now, no matter what her logical, scientific, unreligious mind knew and understood as fact, Kristen was uncomfortable with the subject of demon possession. After her college boyfriend had taken her to watch *Paranormal Activity*, she ended up forcing him to screen a Disney film at home that same night to unwind. When he'd been dumb enough to make a joke about it, modulating his voice to mock her fear, Kristen slapped her boyfriend in the face. In fact, she chose to end their relationship on the spot, though she didn't tell the son of a bitch for a month to avoid sleeping alone.

The memory evoked a peal of nervous laughter from Kristen as she reached to turn off the lamp switch. In a final, desperate attempt to calm down, she turned on some music through her cellphone's speaker. It sounded tinny and unimpressive, but Beethoven's *Moonlight Sonata*, set on repeat, soon proved her best chance to find peace as the noisy house settled. Ludwig took her on a peaceful journey away from all the night's nonsense.

On the cusp of unconsciousness, Kristen felt a silent breeze move a lock of her red curls across her face, and her eyes shot open with uncontrollable panic.

CHAPTER ELEVEN

WHEN TONY ARRIVED AT WORK THAT MORNING, HE heard Kristen Cole speaking on the phone in her bedroom. It was an unexpected sound—she wasn't someone who fancied being out of bed at eight o'clock in the morning. Tony thought something might be wrong, but he didn't have time to ponder the idea before kicking a bucket of dry Plaster of Paris. His clumsy step ensured the container emptied in a terrible mess over the protective plastic on the living room floor.

"Great," Tony mumbled and placed his coffee cup upon the saw table, right where he would've sworn he'd left the bucket yesterday.

He returned to his work truck and retrieved a small hand brush and pan. If he were lucky, Tony could collect enough of it to avoid needing to buy a second container of the product required to redo several pieces of cracked moulding in the main rooms.

Upon re-entering the house, Tony found Kristen by the door, staring at the security keypad beside it.

"Good morning," he said. "Be careful just there; I had a

clumsy accident. Kicked it right over as I arrived, like an idiot. I'll try to get most of it back in the pail."

Kristen didn't respond to him but stopped and stood to the side to let him pass.

"You're up early," Tony said, crouching to sweep the powder. "You have an appointment?"

"I had an awful night," she shook her head.

"Oh? I'm sorry," he replied, nudging the powder to avoid collecting the contaminated layer touching the dirty floor.

"As I was going to sleep, your bucket there fell off the table and scared the hell out of me," Kristen said as life returned to her voice. "I thought someone was breaking in. My nerves were shot by the time I drummed up the courage to come down here and find what it was. I tried to use the security alarm to feel safer, but couldn't get it to work. I just got off the phone with the company, and it turns out Dad canceled the service."

"Darn it—I'm so sorry about the plaster. I can't imagine how it fell from the center of the table." Even if he had left it on edge, Tony didn't see why it would fall in the middle of the night. "He canceled the service?"

"Dad cut it off almost a year ago," Kristen answered. "I suspect he figured he wouldn't need it after Mom died. She probably made him install it."

"Oh, I see," remarked Tony. "So, it's back on now?"

"It will be within the hour. I'll have to go through to reset the code. They sent me the PDF with the instructions," Kristen said, gesturing to the cell phone in her hand. "I'll write the code down for you."

"Cool," he answered, standing up from his chore. He dumped the last of the contaminated plaster in the trash. "I would've brought you a coffee if I'd thought you were up."

"No need. I made a pot in my room a couple of hours ago," she said.

"How'd you manage that?" Tony cocked his head.

"The grocery store in Morro Bay opened at five," said Kristen. "After I never made it back to sleep, I decided to be the first person through the doors when it opened. Found me a sweet little brewer and a bag of Italian roast. Of course, now it feels like I'm walking in a fog, even though I'm high as a kite. Caffeine can't replace actual sleep."

She blinked her eyes and flexed the muscles in her face as if hoping it would clear her vision.

"I'm surprised you didn't buy a pill to put you to sleep," Tony said, now even more annoyed that the plaster bucket had fallen.

"I had pills for that in my purse. Well, NyQuil, anyhow. Didn't work," she all but moaned.

"You're kidding," Tony remarked with raised eyebrows. "I'm usually out in minutes after taking that stuff."

"Me too, except last night," Kristen sighed. "I was doing fine. I'd worked through my anxiety after getting scared. The projector in my head screening serial killer movies was off. I put on soft music to lull me into a trance. But five minutes in, my imagination took over, and I had to turn the lights back on. I tried reading, then watched Netflix on my phone— nothing did the trick. So, around four, I accepted defeat and took a shower. Then I got in the car and drove to buy an overpriced piece of junk so I could wake up for real."

"The sun's up now, so I'll be here to beat up the serial killers. Why don't you try to go down again for a couple of hours?"

"What's the point? I'll never get to sleep with all the noise you'll make, along with whoever is coming today," she replied, unconvinced.

"I've got a few earplugs in the truck that I use for the saw. Fresh ones, of course," Tony offered with a lopsided grin. "I doubt you'll hear anything."

"Don't bother," Kristen shook her head. "I'll make it. If I can hold out until eight tonight, I'll sleep so good I won't wake until late morning."

Tony shrugged his shoulders in defeat. He thought Kristen might fall asleep right where she stood from the looks of her. But who knew her body better than she did?

The phone in the woman's hand released a tone, and she raised it to read the text message that lit up the screen. After typing in a response, the cell phone rang, and Kristen answered it with a smile.

"Good morning," the woman greeted her caller. "No, I'm up early this morning. How's everything coming along?"

Kristen turned and retreated up the stairs to take the call alone. Tony couldn't make out the conversation once she'd gotten upstairs, but he could tell from how her voice raised and giggled that the caller was likely another man.

Well, she's out of my league, he thought, at once pissed over how he'd felt a pang of jealousy. Of course, it didn't matter that Tony knew he didn't stand a shot with Kristen. And sleeping with your boss was never a smart decision. But it still sucked when you wanted something and couldn't have it.

It wouldn't have been much more than a fleeting thought if Kristen hadn't lost her shit with Tony on that first day. The young man couldn't explain it, but being disciplined was a bit of a turn-on for him. At least, it had been with prior girlfriends. Hell, even a teacher had once gotten a rise out of Tony over a science project he didn't take seriously enough. It wasn't as if he sought arguments with women; who in hell wanted to deal with a fight you couldn't land a punch to finish? But Tony sure as hell had something to show off if they went too far. His last girlfriend would use that secret to toy with him. She'd start some shit every time she was in the mood, taking advantage of Tony's condition.

After Kristen had gone in on Tony about not asking the demolition laborers to sweep up their mess, his beta response had opened the floodgates to half a dozen minor problems she harbored with his performance. In fact, Kristen only seemed to let up on Tony when she noticed he was blushing. Perhaps his flushed cheeks convinced the woman to stop herself and recognize how far she was taking the matter. But Tony's face had reddened because a chubby was growing in his jeans. And with all the real estate he had to maintain, it embarrassed Tony to feel the tightening bulge that no doubt placed itself on display.

But it wouldn't happen between them—Tony would be sure of it. The young man wanted this job unlike any he'd ever had, and he wasn't about to jeopardize it over a piece of ass.

He heard Kristen make her way downstairs once she finished her call.

"Tony," she called, "about those earplugs…"

CHAPTER TWELVE

RYAN'S FINGERS TAPPED THE STEERING WHEEL TO THE fast music playing over the car's stereo. He couldn't stop fidgeting in the driver's seat of his black Tesla Model S as he drove through the painfully slow streets of Cambria to collect Kristen for their date.

Ryan was excited to see her again and bring her to the party being held tonight at Hearst Castle. He had told Kristen this morning it was a surprise, but it was important to him she agreed to come, even on such short notice. Ryan had only spoken to her for a few hours during their relationship—once in her father's office and days ago on a proper coffee date. Taken together, those small periods of courtship might appear to be nothing more than a blip to an onlooker, but in the man's eyes, they felt like the start of a grand adventure. Ryan mused he saw a lifetime waiting for him in Kristen's eyes, and he couldn't think of anyone alive he wanted to share this day with more.

His parents had first taken him to Hearst Castle, the notorious former home of news magnate William Randolph

Hearst, when Ryan was a boy. Unlike the museums in San Francisco, Hearst Castle had its art on display as if it were still sitting in someone's home. There were dining halls with the tableware always set and living rooms with table lamps alight for reading from the many sofas. As a boy, Ryan had received many requests from tour guides to please not touch anything, though he loved to sit on the furniture as if he lived there. In fact, Ryan had been so enthralled with the environment that he tested every chair he came across. There was something fantastic about touching sculptures, feeling the swells and grooves of the material as only the master artists ever had.

Ryan had dreamed of living there since his parents first took him to the castle. Those dreams were the fantasies of a boy who could not comprehend the incalculable wealth required to create such a house. But when wealth suddenly and unexpectedly came to Ryan, the museum shouted out from his memory. It was a simple dream that seized his imagination: he would find a way for the money to make a difference.

As a young man, Ryan never thought he would one day devote his time to anything resembling philanthropic work. During his teen years, his parents sacrificed his time to the Church on Ryan's behalf. The forced contributions were lessons on the significance of charity. The boy would have chosen any other way to spend his leisure time. Ryan approached serving meals to the terminally ill or homeless with all the enthusiasm of a root canal. But those acts had seeded an appreciation for the boy's selfless contribution. Both parents were shocked by how their lessons manifested in their son when he enlisted in the U.S. Navy at eighteen.

The young man made the first selfless adult choice of his life just days after the terrorist attacks of September 11th,

2001, in New York City. Ryan told his father it was a sacrifice he needed to make, echoing the horrified man's words years earlier. The same need found Ryan again last year, prompting him to approach his favorite museum with a unique offer. After much coordination, tonight would become another special moment in his life. And that it should happen mere days after he found the woman of his dreams posed as no insignificant coincidence for Ryan. He had lived through enough of life to know that coincidences held divine properties, and he would never dismiss an opportunity such as the one God was handing him.

The car ended its navigation to Kristen's home, where Ryan parked along the front curb. Exiting the car, he reached in the back seat for his blazer and slipped it on, smoothing the fine black silk over his white button-up shirt open at the collar.

The one kink in Ryan's plan was that Kristen likely didn't have any evening wear with her. He had hoped that by calling her in the morning, she might find the desire to go shopping. Ryan had suggested they might photograph Kristen at the surprise event. In his experience, women who knew pictures would be taken at an event went out of their way to look their best. After all, photographs are forever, and bad photographs seem to last even longer.

Ryan had foregone his initial notion of bringing Kristen flowers. For all he knew, the woman was still receiving flowers because of her father's passing. And as badly as he wanted to, Ryan didn't feel it was reasonable to bring any woman jewelry on their second date. He was sure the night's events wouldn't call for ancillary gifts.

Walking up the front path, Ryan saw a young man gathering equipment from an old blue pickup truck. The kid must be the contractor Kristen had mentioned would manage the renovations of her parent's house. When the young man noticed him, Ryan gave a silent nod of acknowledgment and received one in kind.

On the front porch, Ryan rang the doorbell and waited for a response. He looked one last time over at the guy in the driveway. The kid was huge, Ryan thought, with guns bulging like his unit used to sport in the Navy. *Fucker*, he thought to himself, *I'll bet she gets a kick out of that*. Ryan made a subliminal note to up his time in the gym.

He was relieved when Kristen came to the door dressed in a shoulder-less black cocktail dress and heels.

"You look gorgeous," he said, kissing her cheek. When he had greeted Kristen yesterday, Ryan noticed she was unprepared for it. Today, however, she leaned in as if it were natural for her.

"Thank you," Kristen beamed. "Courtesy of my mom's closet. It turns out that Dad kept it just as she left it with him. I hope that's not too much for you to handle. I haven't decided the answer for myself just yet, but I'm leaning towards being okay with wearing her clothes. Mom taught me that a simple black cocktail dress was perfect for every occasion.

"I like that you're wearing it," Ryan answered. "You look beautiful."

"You look beautiful, too," Kristen laughed with relief. "Come in and give me a minute. I'm almost ready."

"Sure," he answered and stepped over the threshold.

"I wouldn't move far from that spot," Kristen warned Ryan as she started up the stairs. "We have a lot of opportunities here for you to ruin your clothes if you're not careful."

"No worries," the man answered her.

The house was smaller than Ryan had figured from the

outside, but he loved the dark, masculine woods covering the walls. At a distance, Ryan could see where the contractor was working on the ceiling mouldings in the dining room. Thoughts of living here passed through Ryan's mind, though he stopped himself from fantasizing just yet. There was so much more going on that required his attention tonight.

From behind Ryan, the young contractor entered through the front door.

"Hey, there," said the kid.

"Hello, I'm Ryan," he said, extending his hand. "Good to meet you."

"Oh, hey, I'm Tony," the young man answered, extending his fist at Ryan. "My hands are all dirty."

Ryan closed his extended palm and returned Tony's offered fist bump.

"It looks like you've already gone to war in here. How's it coming along?"

"Most of it happened the first day when we tore out the bathrooms and kitchen," Tony answered with a relaxed smile. "It's real easy to break shit, but another thing to put it all back together."

"I hear you," said Ryan. "That's the perfect metaphor for life."

Both men heard Kristen's footsteps approach and, in a moment, saw she was wearing a sheer white cover on her shoulders.

"All ready?" Ryan smiled.

"Let's go," she replied and turned to address the contractor. "Will you leave the lights on for me when you go, Tony?"

"No problem," the young man answered. "I'll be on my way out in about an hour."

"Thanks," Kristen replied, and she let Ryan open the front door for her to exit.

When they were down the front path, he opened his passenger door for her, and the pair were soon off.

God, she smells nice, Ryan thought, stealing small glances at her legs.

"Do I get to know what the surprise is now?" Kristen asked, staring at the shifting landscape that passed on their way to the main highway.

"The surprise is forthcoming, I'm afraid, but I can say it lies due north from here," he answered.

The girl gave Ryan a steady look, though he could see he was testing her patience.

"Don't worry. It'll be worth the wait," he promised. "Did you ever get back to sleep?"

When Ryan called in the morning, Kristen had tried to get out of this event. She told him she had trouble getting to sleep and expected to be too exhausted for an outing this evening. But Ryan had begged her to come, pleading with the young woman that it would mean everything if she joined him.

"I got back to sleep after Tony arrived for work," she told him. "Something happened to me last night that never happens: I got scared."

"What do you mean?" Ryan asked with concern.

"A minute after laying down to sleep, a container of his building materials fell downstairs. It made a loud enough sound to trick me into thinking someone was breaking in. By the time I'd worked up the courage to check on it, I was too aware of being alone in that house to go back to sleep."

"I'm so sorry to hear that," said Ryan. "You didn't expect that to happen?"

"I know," answered Kristen, exhaling with frustration. "I said the same thing to myself all night. I felt so stupid. Every time I turned the lights out, I felt something move. Just my breath, no doubt, but then I would turn the lights back on. After a while, I accepted I'd failed to pull the night off and drank coffee to start the new day. If you hadn't called with your invitation, I would've white-knuckled through it until tonight."

"Do you not feel well?" Ryan asked, concerned that she might not be up for this.

"I'm wide awake. That's the weird thing about sleep—if you're deprived but then get a solid eight hours, it's like it never happened. Of course, now my biorhythms are off, so you can keep me out as long as you wish."

"Great," Ryan smiled. "You're gonna have a swell time. I promise."

The car moved north along the highway, which soon came to San Simeon, the small town whose purpose was to serve the museum at the peak of the slopes to the east.

Ryan followed a small service entrance to a shack, where he presented his I.D. to the security guard. When confirmed, Ryan proceeded forward and up the incline leading into the hills where the estate lay.

"Hearst Castle?" she asked.

"The one and only," Ryan answered. "Former home of the richest man in the world. Now a state park and museum. You've never been here before?"

"Never," Kristen confirmed.

"Get ready for a treat," said Ryan.

The road winded back and forth, bringing the car over sharp turns that felt unsafe. Ryan did his best to keep the speed of the Tesla under ten miles per hour when he saw Kristen grab the door handle in apprehension.

"*Where is he taking me?*" Kristen sang in a whisper, eliciting a genuine laugh from Ryan.

Upon topping the first rise of hills, an unforgettable view of the Pacific Ocean confronted them with the last golden rays of the setting sun as it flooded the red sky. Ryan stole a few glances at the breathtaking sight, the stunning light setting Kristen's red hair ablaze before being forced to slam on the car's brakes.

"What are we looking at? Are those... zebras?" Kristen asked in disbelief. Several graceful African animals stood before them to block their advance.

"In fact, they *are* zebras," Ryan answered in his finest David Attenborough impression to Kristen's side-eyed glance. "In the 1920s, Hearst built a zoological park to entertain his guests. When they dismantled the zoo after his death, they rehoused most of the animals in other zoos, but they set several of them free to graze on these hills. A century later, you'll find many unexpected wild animals, including elk, llamas, and, as you can see, zebras, all flourishing here as part of the preserve. Oh, another fun fact: a group of zebras is known as a *dazzle* of zebras."

Ryan's eyes lit up as he smiled like a dorky child.

"That's fantastic," said Kristen, begrudging a smile as she observed the black and white beasts. They were painted in the sun's setting orange glow. "But how are we going to get past them?"

No sooner had she asked when a large tour bus approaching down the hill stopped in front of the disinterested animals. Revving his engine, the bus driver honked his horn at them. After a moment, the magnificent creatures moved off the asphalt onto the grassy earth that sloped down the hill.

When the path was clear, Ryan continued their journey past the bus and up to the sky, where they soon came to a small sign directing them to a special events valet.

"That's what we're after?" Kristen asked.

"I believe so," he answered.

He stopped the car in line behind another pair of vehicles, and a moment later, a valet appeared at her door and opened it to let Kristen out.

"You ready?" Ryan smiled.

CHAPTER THIRTEEN

No matter how enchanting the spot was, Kristen felt nervous. She couldn't remember when she'd been so out of control.

The main entrance to Hearst Castle was a series of wide stone stairways that led up from the driveway to the first of several terraced levels. Ascending the route, Kristen felt insane as she climbed them in heels. Soon enough, Ryan brought them both to a designated reception spot for an outdoor event on the 'Unfinished North Terrace.' They'd filled the massive space with dozens of rounds for dinner, each covered in white linen. They scattered white leather sofas throughout the terrace to create small areas for people to socialize away from their dinner seating. Each element sat upon an expanse of white flooring bathed in purple theatrical lighting. At the center was a black and white checkerboard dance floor, already covered with many couples. A roaring jazz band atop a small stage moved the dancers' feet to an uptempo beat.

Stopping at the check-in desk, Ryan and Kristen waited in a short line behind other arriving guests.

"Is this a black-tie party?" she whispered with concern in his ear and looked at his open collar.

With a sly smile, Ryan scanned the event and whispered back, "I believe so. But don't worry, I'll be fine."

Kristen watched the outdoor room for a hundred details she couldn't commit to memory. She understood from the fragments that this was an assemblage of well-to-do people. Perhaps not so well-to-do that they felt at home in the priceless surroundings of the castle, but then, maybe they did.

"Ryan Hoffman," he told the receptionist, who found his name on her list and spoke it into the small hand radio.

In moments, a tall and handsome gentleman walked up to the couple. Extending his hand to Ryan, he pulled him close to offer an enthusiastic hug.

"I'm so excited you're here!"

The enigmatic man spoke in a velvety southern drawl. At least twenty years older, the man's eyes beamed as if the two were old friends.

"This all looks incredible, John," remarked Ryan. "You've outdone yourself. Let me introduce you to my date. This is Doctor Kristen Cole. Kristen, this is John Steffey—he's the senior curator of Hearst Castle."

"It's a pleasure to meet you," she said, extending her hand with a smile.

"Welcome, Kristen," Steffey said, receiving the woman's hand with unusual affection in his smile. "We're so happy to have you both here tonight. Let me show you to your seats."

Steffey walked through the reception as if he knew where he was taking them among the sea of tables. After snaking around the massive space, they arrived at a table with only three empty seats. Kristen presumed the table was Steffey's own.

"Everyone, this is Ryan Hoffman, who I told you about,

and his friend Doctor Kristen Cole," Steffey yelled over the music that blared from across the dance floor.

Steffey walked around the table one by one to introduce them to people whose names Kirsten forgot at once. When Steffey came to the last people at the table, a middle-aged man and woman, the sight of them shocked Kristen into a doe-eyed look of confusion.

"And this is Governor Newsom and the First Lady, Jennifer," he said with near theatrical reverence.

From his chair, Newsom extended his hand to Ryan and offered words of greeting Kristen couldn't hear. The man's wife only smiled at them both and nodded.

When, at last, they sat down, Kristen came face to face with a sign that read, 'Governor's Table.' A peal of laughter erupted from Kristen, unnoticed by those around them, the sound lost under the band's thunder.

At once, a server approached the couple and asked for their dinner choice, drawing their attention to a small card menu on silver chargers before them.

"I'll have the Caesar salad and the duck," Kristen confirmed for the server and nodded when someone offered champagne.

Electricity surrounded their table. It wasn't just the waitstaff's zealous attention or even the many concentrated glances Kristen and her tablemates seemed to draw from the surrounding eyes. There was a palpable excitement here—as if something important to them was about to happen.

After conversing with Ryan a little longer, Steffey rose from his seat and made his way along the outskirts of the dance floor up to the stage. Giving a simple nod to the conductor, the jazz band drove into the last bars of its number, concluding with a pronounced hit that drew applause from the many couples dancing on the floor.

"Thank you all for joining us on this perfect evening," Steffey's amplified voice shot across the outdoor ballroom, the last purple light of sunset fading behind his back. "Welcome to our annual Hearst Castle Donor's Ball!"

Enthusiastic applause rose from the party guests, who grinned back at the man.

The truth of her surroundings made more sense to Kristen. She felt as if she were sitting in a glamorous wedding reception. *Hopefully, there will be a nice cake*, she mused.

"This has been one of the museum's finest years on record," Steffey told his audience with a generous decorum. "Your incredible support has made it possible for Hearst Castle to expand its offerings to visitors like never before. Your donations ensured we could restore and present a unique collection of fine art this year, one that's remained in storage at the castle since arriving in 1925."

The first course of her table's meal arrived at relative break-neck speed, and Kristen realized the servers had pushed her to order because they were waiting to serve the Governor's table. Kristen reached for her champagne again and again, hoping it would calm her nerves.

While Ryan had implied he was financially successful, nothing about his persona led Kristen to think he would ever choose to be in such a group.

"Does it look good?" Ryan whispered in her ear, gesturing to the salad.

"Everything looks beautiful," she whispered back at him.

"Are you comfortable?"

Kristen gave him a curious smile.

"No. Are you?" she asked, bemused with a wide-eyed look. He had probably meant to inquire if she was warm enough in the evening air, but Kristen couldn't help but make light of the moment.

Ryan flashed his megawatt grin, and the woman's concerns disappeared. He leaned in and gave Kristen an unexpected kiss on the cheek, setting her skin aflame. *Who is this guy?* she wondered, finding herself wrapped in his affections.

Thunderous applause erupted from the room, bringing Kristen back to her surroundings when she realized Steffey had just invited Governor Newsom to the stage. The tall man rose from three seats away, shining his politician's grin on the room when the spotlight landed on him. Newsom soon made his way across the empty dance floor and up to the stage, thirty feet away.

"It's an honor to be here with you all tonight in this place my family and I love so dearly," Newsom said to the contented audience. Many took photographs of him with their cell phones.

"I'm thrilled at the opportunity to tell you about a special surprise the museum will offer on behalf of California's schoolchildren."

Kristen noticed for the first time that Ryan wasn't eating his salad. Instead, he fidgeted with it, seldom watching the spectacle he'd spent so much effort to bring her to.

"It has been a pleasure to join forces with you all in making this year's collection available to the public for the first time since leaving Europe almost a century ago. I'm also happy to announce that one of you has helped us surpass even our most optimistic dreams for this state park. Via a single donation, this private citizen has established an educational grant that will allow for over five-hundred thousand middle- and high school students to visit Hearst Castle for free in the coming year."

Applause erupted from the audience again, cheering with acclaim at Mayor Newsom's announcement.

"This special gift will see attendance in the park almost double. This grant will offer admission, transportation, and meals for California's students in the Los Angeles and Bay Area regions. It will also offer overnight housing and other accommodations for over ten thousand special-needs students and their caregivers."

Again came a riot of applause from the audience.

"I'm delighted to introduce the man who..."

Ryan touched Kristen's arm and leaned in to speak in her ear.

"I have to step away for just a few minutes. Will you be fine here?" he asked.

Before Kristen could comprehend what he'd asked her, the room erupted in applause again, and a spotlight fell on Ryan, setting his golden hair aflame.

He stood from the table and stepped around it on his way to the stage before them.

Kristen forgot to breathe for several seconds once she understood what was happening, that Ryan was the donor Mayor Newsom had advertised in his speech. Though she inhaled again after a moment, she never found the wherewithal to join in the applause that followed Ryan to the podium.

His eyes fixed on transparent panes of glass— teleprompters that displayed the speech only he could see.

"Thank you all," Ryan began when the applause fell away. "I'm honored to be here with you this evening. I first visited Hearst Castle when I was eight, and I'm sure most of you can understand the impression it made upon me. My heart has remained here ever since.

"My mother was a schoolteacher, and I arrived at the museum as a stowaway when she brought her fifth-grade class on a field trip. I was a few years younger than the other kids, which condemned me to spend the trip holding my father's hand. He had taken the day off from work to help my mother when not enough parent chaperones could join her. You might imagine how embarrassing it was for an eight-year-old boy to hold his daddy's hands in front of all those eleven-year-olds. If not, let me assure you I spent the entire day escaping Dad's clutches so I could touch every sculpture and walk on every off-limits rug in the house. Of course, I only did it to impress those teasing fifth-grade girls."

The crowd's laughter pulled Kristen from her daze as it interrupted Ryan.

"What I remember most from that day was when my dad, exasperated with my behavior, pulled me aside and told me I needed to act better because it was an important day for my mother. He explained Mom had paid for most of her students to come to the park because they couldn't afford it. My father's words meant almost nothing to me that day, but I understood from his tone that it was just as important I didn't spoil the day for her with my antics."

Ryan paused as if he was unsure of what he'd say next.

"When my mother passed away, after having spent almost forty years as an educator, my memory of that first trip here and the greater meaning of my father's words rang in my mind. We didn't grow up wealthy. I'm sure all of you here know that school teachers are the lowest-paid professionals in a field where top academic degrees are required. For my parents to have paid for such a trip from the modest neighborhood where we lived would've been a struggle, even if they'd only brought along my sister and me.

"I can't think of anything that would've provided my parents with greater joy than to know that this magnificent park will be available to every California school child within a three-hundred-mile radius. Thank you all for your time, and please enjoy your evening."

As the room applauded, Ryan accepted another handshake from the mayor.

Kristen saw the First Lady mouthing the word 'Congratulations' at her with a sincere nod. It was a surreal salute of approval—as if Kristen should pat herself on the back for doing absolutely nothing. Perhaps she'd soon find herself on a reality television show about the daily lives of dignitaries' wives—the next *Real Housewives* franchise. Kristen would play the psychologist who spent every episode analyzing why her cast members kept shit about each other.

The curator returned to the microphone and advised the room an usher would soon collect them to escort them for a preview of the year's new exhibit. Until then, they were to sit and enjoy their dinners. The band resumed playing as Steffey led the men across the floor and back to their table.

"Everyone," the curator told the table, "I'm going to take us to see the exhibit first, and then they'll serve our plates when we return. Ready?"

Steffey held out his long arms to encourage the remaining table guests to rise and follow him.

Kristen couldn't repress a smile as she rose and accepted Ryan's hand. He escorted her behind the small group, who followed the curator to the terrace's western edge. There, a small staircase descended to an area beneath the party.

CHAPTER FOURTEEN

JOHN STEFFEY LED HIS GUESTS TO A LARGE SPACE beneath the party. It was a similar terrace but oddly hidden under the more massive landing that greeted guests to the estate grounds.

"This little-known space," Steffey began with his grand southern drawl, "was the original entrance to the estate. Hearst decided it was too small to do his vision justice. So, he instructed his architect, Julia Morgan, to build the landing right above us to replace it. They didn't complete the space, which is why we refer to it today as the 'Unfinished Terrace.'"

"We were sitting on the finished end," Ryan whispered to Kristen, who looked at him with puzzlement.

Steffey led the guests along a red carpet that snaked through the dramatically lit space to a pseudo entrance of two Grecian stone pillars. A self-illuminated bronze sign hung between them that read, 'The Palace of Aigai.'

"Built by his father, Philip II, the Royal Palace of Aigai was the childhood home of Alexander the Great," Steffey continued. "Unlike most historical figures who adopted grandiose titles of fame, Alexander remains arguably the most famous conqueror in recorded history. By thirty, he controlled over eighty percent of the known ancient world. Wherever his armies arrived, cities fell under his rule.

"Alexander often sent trophies of spoils home to Macedonia. The result was a collection of artifacts that came to the Palace of Aigai from the corners of three continents. When Greece discovered the palace at the end of the nineteenth century, after being lost for a millennium, government officials sold much of the passed-over contents to international buyers in large lots. William Randolph Hearst was one of the most prolific collectors of Hellenistic antiquities, so he brought several large lots to Hearst Castle in the 1920s.

"When it arrived in California, the curator faced an unusual task. Much of Hearst's purchase was not at all Hellenistic art. Instead, they discovered a unique collage comprising dozens of different cultures and periods. As it was then, and remains still, the challenge of any curator to determine an artifact's origin, Hearst's curator set this lot aside for later in-depth analysis. The lot remained locked in storage for fifty years before another brave curator attempted and failed to accomplish the task during the 1980s.

"I'm very proud to say that after painstaking care, my team and I have been able to catalog every single piece for you. Hearst's efforts from a century ago have resulted in one of the most important multicultural exhibits in the world. I welcome you all to the Palace of Aigai."

The guests gave a small round of applause before Steffey led them through the entrance along the carpeted path. They soon came face-to-face with a colossal bull's head. Its polished horns rose seven feet above it.

"This stunning limestone sculpture is from the Persian capital of Persepolis, where it stood atop a column some fifty feet high. Once the world's richest and most important city, Alexander destroyed Persepolis around 300 BCE, which was an unusual tactic for the monarch. He was famously known for leaving his conquered cities intact. Alexander's usual mark on them was impregnating its royal women to create heirs to rule in his absence. This remains the only known piece of art to survive whole from the reign of Persepolis. It is also the only bull's head of this scale in all of Persian record still bearing its horns intact."

The piece impressed Kristen, but her reaction to this type of art was nothing like Ryan's. He maintained a singular vision as he observed each item they passed. While he remained anchored to Kristen by holding her hand, any onlooker could surmise how he wanted to move through the pop-up exhibition like a child, absorbing each masterpiece in his own time.

They passed Egyptian statues of gods with canine heads, Sumerian reliefs of temples in polished onyx, Chinese warriors covered in gilded jade, and golden Gaelic rhytons covered in gemstones. Also on display was an elaborate selection of jewelry, the ornamentation lit as if Kristen had stepped into daylight. Amulets, scepters, bracelets, crowns, rings, and pieces she couldn't identify, most bathed in gold and composed of the most exquisite gems she had ever seen.

Ryan forced himself upon the curator, who clearly meant to cater to Mayor Newsom and his wife. He interrupted them to ask about piece after piece with an inexhaustible obsession.

"The jewelry was the most difficult undertaking for our team," Steffey confided to Ryan. "A statue can take moments to place, but jewelry requires more investigation. For example, you could attribute these bracelets to a dozen places throughout the Ottoman Empire over a thousand-year period."

Ryan's absorbed eyes poured over each item.

"The journal from our first curator," Steffey noted, "said he was uncomfortable pronouncing them as anything more than modern costume pieces. In the 1980s, when my predecessor attempted to employ radiocarbon dating, she was similarly frustrated when one piece came back as dating over ten thousand years old."

Ryan's eyes lit up, and he tore them from the sparkling stones to look at the curator in astonishment.

"She presumed it was a faulty test," Steffey confided in the spellbound man. "We didn't find the piece in question when we began the project again last year. The notes described it as a diadem thought to be early Persian in design, though it bore few expected telltale markings. In any event, we are all so excited to present this lot, and I'm sure you can see why."

"This is fantastic, John," Ryan agreed, offering a smile composed of all the satisfaction the curator could have wanted to secure from his guests.

Ryan kept Kristen in the exhibition for a little longer than the ushers might have appreciated, but the couple didn't receive more than a polite suggestion; their dinner was ready for service. After exhausting all patience, Ryan asked if Kristen was ready to eat. Receiving her confirmation, he led them back upstairs to their table.

Besides the mayor and guests already seated and eating, another glass of champagne awaited Kristen when she sat. She was grateful to welcome her entrée, which was again served only seconds after her arrival.

"I'm sorry I kept us," Ryan whispered in her ear. "I'm a nerd about that stuff, in case it wasn't too obvious."

Kristen smirked, drawing the wine to her lips.

The men on his side drew Ryan into separate discussions as they ate dinner. Kristen attempted to take part in the chatter near her, but the band drowned out half her words. The isolation became annoying when she finished dinner, and Kristen compensated for it by downing a fourth glass of champagne.

Dropping the flute onto the table, she drew Ryan's attention back to her.

"Would you like to dance?"

"I'd love to," Kristen answered, though it was far from true. She wasn't a fan of this sort of dancing, having no practical knowledge of formal ballroom.

Ryan stood up and pulled Kristen's chair out to take her hand. He led her to the center of the black-and-white checkered dance floor, showing he also knew nothing about dancing. Instead, he held her close to him and rocked them back and forth, pivoting now and then to change their view.

"I'm sorry there's been little opportunity for us to speak on this date," he whispered in her ear. "But I wanted you at my side tonight."

"I'll admit I didn't see any of this coming," Kristen answered. "I didn't even realize you swung with this type of crowd."

"I don't," said Ryan, breathing like he would laugh at the absurd idea. "This is all new to me. One reason I asked you to come was for moral support. Thanks for holding my hand."

Kristen smirked, the champagne settling in her legs. She was grateful their dancing was little more than standing in each other's arms.

"No problem," she answered. "There was a bar, so I'm good to play arm candy for a while. I was taking tips from the First Lady. We might start a TV show together."

"Oh, yeah?"

"It's still up in the air, but I might have to throw a drink in her face and storm off in the first episode. You know, to set up my character properly. I'd like to be the loose cannon with the potty mouth. They have the most fun."

"That seems like a tall order," said Ryan

"I'll be fine, don't worry. I was born for the role, it seems. You'll need to bring me to a few more events like this each year."

"You've got it," he smiled.

"I understand you brought me here to impress me," she whispered. "So, let me set your mind at ease. I'm undeniably impressed."

Ryan drew his cheek close to Kristen's as they danced. She imagined everyone else in the room could see a satisfied smile on his face. They remained on the dance floor through several numbers, taking advantage of the opportunity to speak to each other in private while surrounded by hundreds.

In time, the gala wound down, and the curator thanked the museum's patrons for their continued support. As a special treat, he invited guests to don a nearby staircase to ascend to the Earring Terrace, where they could watch a fireworks show to close the night's festivities. By the time Ryan and Kristen could work their way up to the terrace, it had become chocked full of partygoers, all eager to watch the private display.

Waiting until an usher's head was turned, Ryan slipped Kristen through a velvet rope meant to contain the crowd and whisked her away. Following a darkened path that brought them through a deserted garden, Ryan soon brought his date to an empty terrace that opened to an expanse of sky she would never forget.

Just beneath the romantic iron railing lay a collection of ornamental pools and fountains that flowed downhill to the distance, where the largest swimming pool Kristen had ever seen. Built into the mountainside, it was suitable for hosting an Olympic game, one overseen by Alexander the Great, she mused. The illuminated pool was a Greco-Roman fantasy, with exquisite tile work that patterned through hundreds of square feet of the waveless crystal surface. Dozens of pillars and temple stonework surrounded the whole. Innumerable statues of gods and goddesses stared down at the masterpiece from every conceivable angle.

Kristen thought she recognized it from a Lady Gaga video —something bizarre featuring other artists and Real Housewives. But then, she expected it was a tipsy memory and lent little credence to her silly idea.

"That's Neptune's Pool, and we're standing on his terrace," said Ryan, pointing to the immense marble god who stood carved into the facade of the temple's roof. Above them, the full moon and stars bathed the white stone in their light.

In the far distance, she heard the band on the party terrace strike up a Nat King Cole ballad her father would have loved to hear. From overhead, the first volley of fireworks fired through the sky with a terrible explosion that startled Kristen.

Ryan let go of her hand and drew his date closer to his chest, raising his arm over her shoulders. Kristen appreciated the immediate warmth of his body, shielding her against the night breeze that rose over the mountain to where they stood. After a dozen explosions sent shimmering sparks across the sky in a bouquet of wild colors, Kristen laid her head against his shoulder.

Dropping his arm to her middle back, Ryan embraced her and began a slow dance. He swayed with Kristen long after the distant colored explosions and music had finished.

CHAPTER FIFTEEN

THE NIGHT HAD BEEN LIKE A DREAM, SOMETHING Kristen only expected to watch on a movie screen. They spoke very little on the way home, managing only a sprinkling of conversation.

"I'm surprised all those steps weren't littered with the corpses of women who didn't make it home in their heels," she joked.

Driving home with the black expanse of the Pacific to their right, soon leaving the highway for the winding streets hidden beneath towering pine trees, Kristen felt like she was floating. The delicious champagne still sailed through her bloodstream.

How to make this sensation never end?

But Kristen knew it was all too perfect to trust. The man would no doubt ask for an invitation inside her home, and who could blame him? Kristen had done far more for far less in her time. But perhaps this was the man for whom she should follow the venerated protocols of courtship. Wasn't that how it was supposed to be done? Keep an eager man at bay until he placed a ring on your finger?

Kristen couldn't fathom such a thing, its tones of misogyny slicing through the notion, and she decided Ryan would find himself in her bed that night.

Pulling up to the house, Ryan rose from his seat and made his way around to open his passenger door, holding out his hand to help Kristen stand.

When they arrived at the home's front porch, illuminated by the lamps that Tony had left on at Kristen's request, she placed her key into the door and opened it. She then turned to Ryan as if she would bid him goodnight.

"Well, thank you for an unforgettable time," she said with a coquettish grin, prepared to ask him inside.

In a silent move, Ryan lifted his hand to her jaw and drew her face to meet his lips. Alone now, his kiss came with more sensual force. Not too much, but just enough wet invasion to show Kristen the truth of his desire and need for her.

She soon brought her hand over Ryan's shoulder like they might dance again. But the lovers' feet remained still on the porch as they enjoyed each other's touch without the slightest hurry. Who could say how long they stayed there? Kristen only knew how sweet he tasted and how right he felt.

"Come inside," she whispered in his ear when they stopped.

Ryan seemed contemplative over her invitation.

"Another night," he whispered, kissing her one more time before withdrawing from Kristen, bidding her goodnight before he started back down the path to his car.

Kristen was more than surprised by his refusal—she was shocked. Admittedly, this was a first for Kristen to have a man decline such an invitation. But more than the feelings of concern she felt, Kristen was at once wrought with a startling hunger to have Ryan. Was this what her college roommate had meant when she told Kristen to make a man work for it?

"Don't just give it away when you're ready. Make them wait for it," the girl had told Kristen. "If you make out with a guy, but hold back the goods, it'll drive him crazy. He'll do anything for you."

The girl hadn't mentioned that this technique worked both ways. Kristen had never been so turned on in her life. She had to temper her breathing as she attempted to focus on arming the security system. She typed her code into the pad with distinct concentration to get it right. Kristen stole upstairs for bed when the device beeped the perimeter was armed.

Unlike the previous night, she wasn't concerned about being alone. Whether it was the champagne or her arousal or having found herself refused by a man, Kristen couldn't have entertained such fears if she had tried.

Out of pure habit, Kristen hung her mother's dress in the closet. She removed her bra and slipped on an oversized t-shirt. Kristen didn't bother with her hair and soon slipped into her bed, feeling the weight of sleepiness fall upon her. Oh good, she thought to herself upon realizing sleep had come, extinguishing her earlier concerns of having disrupted her bio-rhythms.

As sleep took over, Kristen clung to flashes of Ryan, the sublime sensation of his lips and tongue. She fantasized fleetingly over having that tongue between her legs. The sweet dream played over and over in her mind.

Ryan again held her in his arms while they swayed to the music. The cool breeze of the evening blew through her hair, lifting the red satin curls. The brisk cold made Kristen feel the warmth of his body all the more. She thought of love. Kristen felt the need to love this man and embraced his sublime adoration as it enveloped her.

"I feel such relief with you here in my arms," Ryan said. "I didn't know if I would ever feel such compatibility again."

"I've never felt this," Kristen answered. "It's as if the past means nothing to me. I can't even remember any of it."

"Will you let me love you?" Ryan asked and brought his warm lips to taste her.

Kristen surrendered to his kisses, giving Ryan what he needed from her. Indeed, she realized how deeply she needed it, withholding nothing from him as he devoured her. Her body felt alive, and in time, she broke away to whisper in his ear.

"Please?"

Ryan bent to bring his forehead to hers, and they continued to sway to the band's sweet jazz.

"Come with me," he whispered.

In moments, they found their way to a bed; she couldn't say how. It didn't matter to Kristen.

He undressed her, removing each article of clothing from her, releasing Kristen's white skin to the quiet breeze of an overhead fan. She felt no cool now, only the radiating heat of his body as she pulled at his shirt and pants, letting them fall away.

Kristen fell back on the bed and received Ryan's warm lips again. They were insatiable and couldn't draw enough wet love from her. Ravenous, his mouth found its way to her neck, and Kristen sighed in delight to feel his warm breath on her skin.

His hands raised to hold her breasts, and she responded with near delirium at the sensation, giving way to his mouth's intense sucking on her nipples. Soon drawing them to become hard, Kristen squirmed to feel his unforgiving tongue lap at her chest. She was powerless to stop him, not that she would dare to.

With unexpected force, Ryan lifted both her legs. His hands braced Kristen by the crook of her knees so that her hips and back pressed into the pillow, exposing her sex. Kristen let out a small gasp at the change. She glanced long enough to see the intense look of greed in his eyes before Ryan's tongue fell between her legs, licking her in one long pull like a lion with its prey.

Kristen couldn't contain the small sounds of excitement she released over being so helpless within Ryan's control. She sensed he loved the sounds as his eyes raised again to look at her with a beam of pleasure. Letting his breath torture her for a moment with chills as it cooled her, Ryan set about on her sex with a ravenous tongue.

Kristen squirmed as he drew the fire out of her. He locked onto his prize, forcing her hips to rock in delighted frustration. On and on, Ryan dined with a singular focus, lapping at Kristen mercilessly. It proved a futile plea when she whispered for him to wait. The fire of her climax obliterated all reason to speak. Kristen's release took control of her every thought, and she rode each scalding wave that took hold, bringing hard fits of contraction.

At some point, Kristen knew Ryan had released his grip on her legs. The understanding found her when she felt his torso lay down on her, the man's head falling beside her, and his lips finding her ear lobe to draw it into his mouth. With unmistakable pressure, she felt Ryan's cock enter her, evincing small cries as she relaxed to accommodate him. The tingling throughout her sex from her orgasm kept a hold over Kristen, and the sensation was sublime.

"I love you," he whispered, his mouth sucking on her earlobe.

Kristen felt the same and turned her face to find those lips again. She drew them to her and let the symphony of pleasure sing through her every fiber.

Opening her eyes to find Ryan's handsome face, Kristen saw two dark sapphire-colored eyes watching her from beneath dark, heavy brows. His eyes were too beautiful, liquid orbs of sharp color that the growing morning light of the room illuminated like jewels. The desire they held for her was unmistakable—rich and coveting.

Kristen felt the dream slipping away. As consciousness arrived more and more, she realized she was dreaming. Knowledge beyond their immediate passion crept into focus, and Kristen realized it was not Ryan who made love to her. Each fragment of pleasure that pumped through her body soon became a part of the material world.

For one distinct moment, Kristen understood she was awake. The handsome man's warm steel deep within her body filled Kristen with a glorious pleasure. And then, as if her mind wouldn't accept another moment of it, he disappeared. His face vanished. The weight of his body ceased to press down on her. The girth of his cock was no longer present within her, and she felt her sex close in response to its absence.

Kristen jolted from the shock, moving backward to crash against her bed's headboard, where she screamed in terror.

CHAPTER SIXTEEN

DOCTOR LISA KATH WAS A SHORT WOMAN WITH A KIND face and more than a bit of quirky humor in her eyes. She acknowledged this at the beginning of their session and divulged how she sometimes struggled to temper it for her clients. Kristen sat in the woman's office, unprepared to speak to a stranger. No one understood the full ramifications of discussing sensitive problems with a therapist better than another therapist.

"Take your time," Lisa said when Kristen didn't want to speak.

She hadn't asked for a recommendation while searching for a counselor. Instead, Kristen found the first woman with a website citing availability for new patients. It was a first for Kristen, and going out of her way to locate a woman exposed a prejudice she had not been fully aware of until today.

"Are you part Filipina?"

The sting of embarrassment Kristen felt while the words left her mouth was debilitating. *I'm asking strangers about their ethnic heritage while I stall for courage*, Kristen thought.

Lisa's eyes widened with a comic smile.

"Yes, I'm half," she gushed. "Dad was a third-generation Anglo-American, and he married Mom when the Navy stationed him in the Philippines."

"Were you born there? Or did she emigrate before they had you, or..."

Lisa suppressed a burst of laughter.

Kristen did a double-take, unsure of what had happened.

"What?" Kristen asked.

"I'm sorry, it's just... It struck me as funny, is all," Lisa offered, stifling her laughter.

"What do you mean?" Kristen asked, unwilling to drop her guise.

"Well, you're a therapist, right?" Lisa asked with a suspicious slant.

Kristen exhaled, frustrated with herself.

"No, it's fine, really," Lisa promised. "But you're a doctor of psychology and a working therapist, so there's no doubt in my mind you understand what's going on right now. You're stalling, which is fine. Get there when you're ready. It's just that you're spending two-hundred-fifty dollars an hour to ask me if I can cook lumpia," she remarked, shaking her head, trying to find some levity. "I wasn't ready for that one. And then I got the 'church giggles' because I realized how inappropriate it was for me to laugh."

The patient allowed herself to smile, which felt rather good despite the sting of embarrassment she felt.

"You know, I heard myself ask you that question, and..." Kristen shook her head before letting it fall forward.

"I guarantee you I'm taking this seriously," Lisa added. "I wouldn't disrespect you in that way."

Kristen nodded her head but remained quiet.

"You must be so caught off guard by whatever brought

you here. It's not like you don't see your assigned therapist in San Diego," Lisa added, examining the pre-interview form Kristen had filled out before the session started.

"I know exactly how this works, and I understand what it seems like," Kristen assured the woman.

"Perfect, so let's make the most of it," Lisa encouraged. "Just blurt it all out, and let's go from there. Rip the Band-Aid off as fast as you can. I've got your back."

Kristen stopped, nodding her head, feeling the fear return. She raised her eye and stared at Lisa, wanting to do as the woman suggested: say it as fast as possible.

"I'm terrified," Kristen said, though her voice failed her, the words spoken like a whisper.

"What has you so terrified?" Lisa asked, her eyes becoming distressed by the unmistakable fear in Kristen's voice.

"I had an experience the other day. Well, more than one, I realize now," Kristen announced with unnecessary correction.

"What kind of experiences?"

Kristen stared at the woman again, wanting to scream the words but struggling to find a better way to say them.

"Hallucinations," Kristen admitted.

"What did you hear or see?" Lisa asked, nodding to assure the woman she was prepared for the truth.

"Okay," Kristen began. "The first time, I thought I was dreaming. I would still think I was dreaming if I hadn't had the other experiences. I dreamt that my home contractor would come to my room and speak with me. He told me he was waiting for me. Then he asked if I would let him love me."

"Do you have an intimate relationship with the man?"

"Not at all," Kristen clarified. "I'd known the guy for maybe a few days. Purely a professional relationship."

"Okay," Lisa acknowledged, nodding for Kristen to continue.

"The man in the dream looked like Tony—that's my contractor's name—but he was very different. He spoke to me with such intimacy, and Tony would never have done such a thing. Then I touched Tony, and when I looked up again at him, the dream changed, and in place of Tony was another man's face."

"Whose face?" Lisa asked, prompting Kristen when she again became silent.

"I don't know," Kristen answered. "I've never seen the other man before. But the face startled me, and I woke up in a panic."

"Because you were scared?"

"No, I wasn't scared the first time. I was startled because it was an unexpected change," Kristen clarified.

"He was just a man you didn't know?"

"Right. And this man wasn't intimidating, just unexpected."

"But you thought it was a dream, and now you feel differently? What changed your mind?"

"The next time I remember dreaming, the same man took the place of another man I was with," answered Kristen.

"The same scenario?"

"It was very different," Kristen explained. "For instance, it was an erotic dream. I was making love with the man I'm seeing. And then at the end, when I looked at his face, I found the other man's eyes staring back at me."

"The man you don't recognize? He was the person you were having intimate relations with in the second dream?"

"Not at first, but near the end, yes. It was the same man," Kristen confirmed.

"How elaborate were these dreams? Do you remember more about them than how they made you feel?" Lisa's brow began to furrow.

"Thoroughly elaborate. The first one is still very clear, though I thought little about it then," Kristen acknowledged.

She lowered her head as if unsatisfied by her statement.

"That's not true," she began again. "It was impactful because I was bothered by how it exposed my feelings for Tony, which I didn't want to examine."

Lisa nodded again as if to give Kristen license to say what needed to be admitted.

"Tony's a carpenter, and he's working to restore my parent's home," Kristen began again. "That's how his employer should describe him. However, your best girlfriend might also describe him as a twenty-four-year-old Adonis with the kind of body they print on fitness beefcake magazine covers."

"Oh," Lisa blinked. "And that's the part you didn't want to confront? That was part of the dream?"

"Right," Kristen acknowledged reluctantly. "The dream was hot and heavy, and I became aroused. That part threw me."

"Because you're attracted to him," Lisa elaborated on her understanding. "But acting on those feelings is inappropriate in your position. Then you were embarrassed by it when the feelings manifested in the dream?"

"Right."

"So, both dreams were erotic in nature? What was the third dream?"

"No, there were only two dreams," Kristen corrected the woman. "In between them, I had a separate event happen where I experienced a minor panic attack because I thought someone was breaking into my home."

Lisa raised her eyebrows in concern.

"The whole time this was happening, I was checking myself," Kristen stressed to assure her therapist. "Something fell on the house's ground floor and made a sharp noise. It scared me for a minute, but I got out of bed and checked on it. I was scared shitless but determined everything was fine, and went back upstairs to bed. I tried to calm down and return to sleep, but I couldn't. Each time I got close, I felt like something was moving in the room, so I turned the lights on to check in a panic. It was just miserable the whole night, and I never made it to sleep until the sun came up. I tried sleeping with the lights on but didn't want to close my eyes. I had to wait until the damned contractor came to work so I could feel safe enough to sleep."

"Tony?"

"Yes," Kristen rolled her eyes against her will, mortified by the connection at which Lisa hinted.

"And then you had the sex dream about the man you're seeing? What's his name?"

"I'm seeing Ryan," answered Kristen.

"Tony and Ryan," the therapist mouthed while jotting down notes.

The thought of their names ending up on the woman's notepad made Kristen cringe, but she understood the woman's purpose and exhaled in resignation.

At once, Lisa looked up from her notes at Kristen.

"So, you've not had sexual relations with Tony, but you have with Ryan?" Lisa pointed for clarification.

"No, I haven't had sex with Tony and don't intend to, but I haven't had sex with Ryan either. Our relationship just began, and he's decided he wants to take it slow. Slower than I care to, anyhow."

"I'm with you," Lisa prompted when Kristen didn't continue. "I'm just waiting for you to explain why you think the dreams were hallucinations."

Kristen stared off aimlessly as if contemplating how to say it.

"The second dream was... massive. It felt as if I were awake the whole time. I saw, smelled, and tasted every sensation. It was so elaborate that until I woke up, I felt completely lucid."

"Do you normally remember your dreams in such detail?"

"Rarely ever," Kristen declared. "Even when I wrote them down in a dream journal during college, they were little more than weird and pointless situations. At best, they were funny. I remember nightmares far more concretely, but I don't remember their details as much as I recall the fear they inspire. I'm not accustomed to fearing real things. Sure, I'm scared of a serial killer breaking into the house to rape and murder me, but it's not an irrational fear. I don't worry about it actively. I lock the doors at night, but I probably have a better chance of dying in a plane crash than meeting up with a serial killer in the middle of the night."

Lisa nodded as if she agreed with the observation.

"I don't like movies about demon possession. I sneaked a look at *The Exorcist* when I was barely ten years old, and it did a number on me. In fact, many of the nightmares I've had in my life revolved around the Devil taking control of me. I've had that conversation with my regular analyst a few times over the years. That's one irrational fear that takes a bit of focus to still defeat as an adult."

"I've heard that from several people in our field," Lisa

nodded. "I think that's perfectly reasonable, frankly. I've never wanted to work with the heaviest diagnoses for the same reason. Honestly, I don't know how doctors find the strength to work with patients in that state. I think they're heroes."

Kristen nodded in agreement.

"I've come close, but I've always ended up transferring the patient because I've been unable to concentrate on my job," Kristen admitted.

"I get it."

Kristen leaned forward as if preparing to say what she had been fighting throughout the session. She looked into Lisa's eyes and thought she saw a glimmer of focused recognition.

"When I saw the man, the one I don't recognize, he was flesh and bone. Even though I was dreaming, I knew in the dream that I was dreaming, and I saw him through that level of awareness. Then, as the dream progressed, at some point, I was awake. Like I am right at this moment. It was morning, and early dawn light filled the room. I saw him as clearly as I see you sitting in that chair. Except he was in my arms. He was inside of me. We were making love, and then he disappeared in little more than the blink of my eye, and I couldn't feel him anymore."

Lisa's face became lifeless as she stared at Kristen. In time, her expression changed to acknowledgment.

"And it was the same man from the dream with Tony days before?"

Kristen nodded.

Lisa looked down at her notes and then again at the answers Kristen had written on the standard questionnaire.

"Are you about to say you think the man in your dream, and then in your waking moments, was a demon?" The therapist spoke with emotionless precision.

"I used the word 'ghost' to describe it to myself, but I suppose that's semantics," Kristen answered.

Lisa appeared to receive the answer heavily, a tinge of pain breaking her guise.

"Kristen, you're a doctor of psychology," Lisa announced with kind frankness, "a scientist—

"So, I must know everything you're about to tell me," Kristen interrupted the woman.

Lisa exhaled and extended her hand to Kristen, inviting the patient to diagnose herself.

"The patient has recently experienced the traumatic loss of a loved one, a parent, coming little more than a year after her other parent died," Kristen began. "Within days of her loss, the patient experienced increased levels of stress due to financial concerns and the actions she needed to take to resolve them, which included home renovation, two of the most stressful influencers. The patient experienced these stressors while being forced away from her home and established support system. Additionally, the patient has experienced inconsistent sleep and heavier-than-normal caffeine consumption mixed with sleeping aids and alcohol."

Lisa nodded and signaled for more.

"Because the patient has never demonstrated the symptoms in the past and has only experienced them over a grieving period of fewer than six months, she does not qualify for any variety of schizotypal attribution. The experienced hallucinations are more soundly attributed to the pharmacological reaction prompted by mixing stimulants with depressants, both consumed during bouts of mild sleep deprivation."

Lisa nodded with pursed lips as if every word Kristen spoke was dead-on.

"I wrote everything on Axis IV in my mind and sent the

patient off to exercise and sleep properly," Kristen added with a whisper.

Lisa smiled, relieved her patient understood what had happened to her.

"I thought perhaps if I came here today and said it aloud, the fear would disappear, and I'd feel better," Kristen mused.

"And do you feel better?"

After a moment, Kristen sighed and nodded.

"If I didn't have to report the hour, I'd give you a discount," Lisa said, shrugging her shoulders and offering an expanding grin.

Kristen laughed, feeling the tension leave her back.

"Do you want to talk about either of the men you mentioned? We could explore your attraction to Tony or why you think Ryan wants to postpone intercourse."

Kristen scoffed.

"It's not a real problem. Ryan hinted he wants to take it slow, that's all. It was only the second date. And I invited him into it my dead father's home, who he used to work with."

Kristen shook her head again.

"Okay, but I still feel bad for him," Lisa chimed. "How's he ever going to deliver like your imagination does? The poor bastard. Do you want to work on that?"

WHAT KRISTEN TOLD THE COUNSELOR WAS TRUE: SHE felt better. But knowing why an experience happens to you doesn't stop it from happening. It merely gives you an edge toward resolution. Yes, she'd have to start exercising, but she'd also need to stop the NyQuil and alcohol, at least for now.

Kristen pondered how to get through the night as she drove toward the highway entrance to return home. The solution presented itself at once, and she looked in her mirror to pull over her car. It was such a simple answer. She'd recommended it to at least a hundred of her patients.

After searching her phone's internet browser, Kristen found a website for the local pet shelter.

CHAPTER SEVENTEEN

TONY HEARD KRISTEN'S SEDAN PULL INTO THE driveway as he finished cleaning up the worksite to prepare for going home. When she'd left this morning, his boss had uttered little more than a tepid greeting. It gave Tony his first real taste of what it would be like when Kristen drove home to San Diego and left him alone to manage the site.

So far, everything had gone far smoother than he expected. The bumps in the road had been manageable, and Tony was far more confident he could manage the subcontractors. In fact, Tony was optimistic that, if need be, he could hire the contractors on his own. Every scholastic point he knew about home remodels had proven to be on-point, and he no longer hesitated to discuss matters with each worker when they didn't execute a task to his standards.

A cacophony of high sounds came from Kristen as she moved up the driveway and around to the rear yard. She sounded as if she were speaking to a rambunctious toddler.

"Yes! We're home! Yes! Good girl! Wait! Wait! Ah, ah, ah! Sit! Yes! Yes! Sit! Good *guuur*!!"

Tony walked to the kitchen at the back of the house and

looked through the glass door to see Kristen unleashing an adult Husky with a light smoke overcoat, white underbelly, and crystal blue eyes. The animal wagged her curled fluff of a tail as if she were the happiest dog in creation.

Tony loved dogs, but Huskies held a special place in his heart. He'd been raised with them, his family owning six dogs when he was a kid. Tony couldn't remember a night back home when less than two cuddled against him in his bed at night. Of all the changes that came with adulthood, not having the space to keep a pet was the hardest challenge, especially when he moved onto the bus.

Tony opened the glass door and entered the backyard, drawing the dog's attention. The Husky paused until she saw Tony drop to his knee and beckon her to him, then ran like the wind to cover him with wet kisses.

"Isn't she beautiful?"

"What a sweetheart!" Tony answered, more to the Husky than his boss.

"Her name is Penelope, and she's two years old," Kristen confirmed.

"Hello, Penny, my love. Oh no, your poor owner," Tony said as she shook with a joy that seemed to make her weak at the knees.

Placing the animal's front legs on his shoulders, Tony invited Penelope to shower him with the tongue bath she was desperate to deliver. The attention continued for some time, developing into deep belly rubs as she swayed atop the grass, in clear heaven from his reciprocal affection.

"Well, don't let me stand in the way between the two of you," Kristen joked at their mutual adoration.

"Are you watching her for a friend?" he asked while massaging the animal into perfect joy.

"Nope, she's all mine," Kristen declared. "I just adopted her from a shelter."

"What?" Tony asked, his focus pulling away from the animal to recognize the woman's statement.

"I thought this was the right time for me to have a dog, and when I got there, she was so alert and happy to see me. We fell in love," Kristen smiled again.

"I'll bet," Tony responded, giving Penelope a hard pat on the butt to signify their communion was over. "Go play, Penny! Go, play!"

The dog sprang to her feet with almost supernatural precision and tore off through the backyard.

Tony rose when Penelope was off and scrunched up his nose with indecision. He didn't know if he should discuss the matter with Kristen, but the words left his mouth before he could debate it.

"Don't you live in an apartment in San Diego?"

"It's a condo conversion, but yes," she said, smiling as the joyful animal flew through the half-acre of grass and bushes, exploring at breakneck speed.

Again, Tony scrunched his face, unsure what to say.

"It's tough to keep a Husky in an apartment," he said, trying to keep his voice from rising. "Did they tell you about the breed when they gave her to you?"

"They said she'd be perfect for me. I told them I needed a dog to exercise with. I need to get back into my fitness routine, especially after all the depression I've been going through. They said she's great for jogging."

"Oh, yeah, for sure," Tony nodded. "At that age, more like running for miles and miles. A few times each day."

"It won't be that bad," Kristen smirked. "Once she gets the excitement for her new home out of her system, I'm sure she'll be just fine."

No sooner had Kristen answered when Tony realized Penelope was gone. Unlike the homes in California's major cities, a feature of living in this section of Cambria was that home lots, lying under canopies of massive pine trees, were separated by nothing more than the forest itself. Beyond the cut grass and flowerbeds that Richard and Margaret Cole had maintained around their wooden deck was an untouched forest floor running up the steep hillside.

"I'm afraid her ancestors have called her away," Tony remarked.

"Penelope?" Kristen yelled out, then waited for the Husky to show.

Tony shook his head in disbelief at her expectation.

When Kristen hollered twice without receiving the slightest reply from the dog, she stepped on the edge of the pavement, looking down at the grass with apprehension.

"I won't make it far in these," Kristen said, gesturing to the black heels she wore with her jeans. "Would you call her to me?"

With a look of disbelief, Tony paused before reaching for the leash Kristen held. He moved to the yard's edge and whistled into the forest, where he could only see about a hundred feet.

"Penny!" he yelled, following the dog's name with a couple more whistles.

Exhaling in agitation, Tony advanced through the shrubbery encircling the yard and stepped onto the earth of the forest floor.

CHAPTER EIGHTEEN

KRISTEN FELT LIKE AN IDIOT AS SHE WATCHED THE contractor take off into the trees. She had let Penelope off her leash with the unfounded presumption that the dog would stay nearby.

As she waited, Kristen realized that neither would return soon. *Son of a bitch*, she thought to herself. Feeling useless, Kristen returned to her car and retrieved the paperwork and small bag of food provided by the rescue kennel.

She examined the paperwork, attempting to remember the duties she'd need to complete when she got home. Holding up the small bag of food, Kristen scanned the instructions, which announced she could add warm water to give her dog a special treat.

Kristen hadn't owned a dog since her father bought her a puppy when she was nine. But her experience lasted less than a month after she'd failed to uphold a laundry list of promises to care for the little guy. After he'd urinated on every surface within three weeks, and Kristen's mother had stepped in droppings not once but two times, the adorable Golden Retriever vanished. She'd never gotten a satisfactory answer for where the puppy had gone, but her parents had established a new rule in its name to make sure Kristen could never have one again.

In the following years, Kristen found herself in place after place that prohibited pets; first in college, then in apartments she shared with roommates, and then while living with boyfriends who were against the idea of committing to a surrogate child. By the time Kristen lived alone, the thought of a dog never crossed her mind.

From a distance, she heard their feet trotting through the refuse of the forest floor. When Tony and Penelope emerged back into the rear yard, the animal was again excited to see Kristen as if they had been apart forever.

"Oh my god, Tony, thank you," she said with relief.

"She's thirsty," he said. "Where's her bowl?"

Kristen blinked but didn't respond. She turned to the house as if her mind were searching for a bowl in the kitchen that was no longer there.

Tony offered a look of confusion at Kristen's silence.

"They gave me coupons for Petco, but I haven't gone yet."

"Why not?" Tony asked her with concern.

"I thought I'd go tomorrow. They gave me some food, so there's no rush."

"That's a sample," Tony clarified, frustration coloring his voice. "That's good for one meal. What's she gonna eat in the morning?"

When Kristen's answer didn't come, Tony exhaled sharply.

"Hold her," he said, handing the leash to Kristen. "Don't let go of that."

Tony stomped away, not quite masking the expletive that left his voice as he turned the corner toward the side driveway. Kristen couldn't be sure, but it sounded like he said, "...fucking kidding me."

What the hell was that? Kristen thought, astounded by the man's attitude.

After some time, Tony returned to the yard with two small plastic buckets, upon which he turned the garden hose to clean. They appeared to be used plaster buckets. Tony shook one of them dry and filled the other with fresh water.

Penelope pulled on her leash, determined to go to him, but Kristen held tight to the dog's leash as ordered.

"I found her three homes down drinking from your neighbor's pool," he said, placing the bucket of water near the deck railing. He gestured with his hand for Kristen to walk Penelope over to him.

With an almost violent sound, the dog lapped at the water with insatiable thirst.

"I'm surprised she's still so thirsty," Kristen said.

"I stopped her just as she began," Tony clarified. "You'll have to be more careful. She'll get sick from the chlorine the same way we would."

"I'm sorry I let her go," Kristen replied, though it wasn't much of an apology. "I didn't think through how there's no fence out here."

"It wouldn't matter," Tony returned. "A fence couldn't contain her. You saw how she moves. She has to be trained on what her limits are."

With that, Tony opened the rear glass door and walked into the house, shutting it too loud for Kristen's comfort. Remaining still for the dog, who continued to lap away until the bowl was half empty, anger took hold of her, and she started to count. The conciliatory viewpoint she'd offered moments earlier disappeared, and Kristen felt herself grow warm. *1, 2, 3, 4, 5, 6, 7, ...*, she thought, attempting to relax. If Kristen went after Tony now, she'd tell him to fuck himself.

She'd have to talk to him, but it didn't call for more than a simple notice about his attitude. As she counted, Kristen felt herself become calmer. And when Penelope had sated herself, they crossed the deck to head inside the house.

The dog's feet tapped frantic steps on the exposed concrete floor of the kitchen as she entered the house.

"No. No. No!" Tony said firmly to the dog. "Back up. Outside. Now!"

Moving only an awkward step backward, Penelope jumped up and down, enthralled to be inside this house that smelled just like her humans.

"Penny, sit!" he exclaimed, with no response from the dog.

Kristen pulled back somewhat on the dog's leash but was unprepared for Tony's reaction to their entering the kitchen. In a swift move, he took the leash from Kristen and walked the animal back to her water near the deck railing.

"Up here!" Tony shouted, and he drew his hand to his face, holding his index finger along the slope of his nose.

With what Kristen observed as a supernatural effect: the dog stopped her raucous movement to stare at attention.

"Sit *down*," he said to her.

She lowered her rear to the ground with mirrored, calm determination, never taking her eyes from him.

"All the way down," Tony continued, and Penelope's front legs went out like clockwork, lowering her entire frame to the floor. "Stay down."

Tony unfastened the dog's leash and looped it around the railing before reattaching it to her collar so she couldn't run off.

"Whoever had her before put her through basic training," Tony said as he reentered the house.

His undeniable ability to control Penelope impressed Kristen, but his behavior outraged her.

"Why did you do that?" she closed the door behind them. All calm had left her voice.

"She obviously can't come in here. Look at this shit," Tony said with even less patience, gesturing to the demolished room with its missing floor and exposed wiring. "She'll get hurt."

"Obviously, she's coming inside," Kristen answered, mimicking his earlier impertinence, the word still stuck in her craw. "I'm surprised her champion thinks I'm going to have her sleep outside alone."

Tony shook his head with consternation.

"You'll have to keep her in your room," he replied. "Take her through the front door and keep her on her leash while she's not in your room. Make her stay on the paper path the whole time."

"You know, if you'd just clean up this site for once, there wouldn't be any problem," Kristen returned, raising her voice. "Look at all this garbage everywhere. I get it's a worksite, but you don't have to leave all your crap lying around. Why is that wiring exposed, anyhow? You couldn't even put tape on it?"

"It doesn't matter if I tape it," he shot back, "the power isn't on in this room. She'd bite down on the wires to chew them off. She'd bite everything in the room that would fit her mouth. God knows what she'd swallow. Have you never had a dog before?"

"Yes, I've had a dog before," Kristen wailed, the sting of his question affecting her more than she expected. "You're the one who slapped her hind and told her to run off. That's not what this is about. You need to stop talking to me in that tone, or you need to get the fuck out of here. Now, do whatever the hell you need to do to make the house safe for the both of us, the stuff you should already have done by now, and then you can go home."

Kristen stormed off through the kitchen and into the dining room, her heels pounding before she stopped and turned back.

"And if you hit her in the butt again like that, you'll lose that hand!" Kristen shouted, turning to the stairs.

When the woman made it to the upstairs landing, her heavy breathing had little to do with the exertion of climbing twenty steps. Placing her hand on the door handle, Kristen stopped to realize Tony had followed her up the stairs. Astonished, she turned to see him approach in anger.

"First, this is an active worksite," Tony said, his deep voice lowered to almost a whisper, "and there's nothing I can do to change that until she's finished. Second, we both know you couldn't care of a houseplant, much less that dog. There's no way you've ever been responsible for a breathing animal before and still must be told she requires food and water to live."

As Tony approached Kristen to stand less than a foot before her, she could smell his deodorant fighting against his long workday. The scent repelled her as much as it attracted her. Kristen's skin became alerted to the heat of his frame as it emanated through the small space between them.

"And if I ever slap your ass like Penny's, you'll fucking thank me for it."

CHAPTER NINETEEN

TONY LEFT KRISTEN BEFORE SHE DRIFTED OFF, returning to her room only to bring Penelope upstairs.

"Go to mommy," he whispered to the dog, who jumped into bed and took Tony's former place beside Kristen. He bid them both goodnight and shut the door before leaving.

Eight hours later, Kristen awoke, having slept as soundly as she could remember.

She had been unprepared for how Tony approached her the prior evening, but the woman hadn't offered so much as a look of protest when the young man reached out to draw her to him. Their engagement had been intense, filled with resentful anger that realized itself through something just short of erotic violence. They had grudge-fucked each other, and as Kristen rose from bed to go to the bathroom, she felt the unmistakable soreness between her legs. The pain was not so much the result of his exertions, though Kristen learned that Tony's body was not a mirror athlete last night. Instead, Kristen's ache came from how the young man's cock was too large for her.

Margaret Cole had once laughed at Kristen and her

girlfriends when she overheard their slumber party commentary. They'd all agreed their ideal boyfriend must have a huge penis.

"Ladies, don't be too eager to measure a lover's worth with a ruler," Margaret had told them, embarrassing Kristen with her openness and entertaining the other young girls with her commentary on their racy topic. "Every man comes in a different size because every woman also comes in a different size. The genuine challenge of finding the most suitable man, ladies, is finding the right size penis for your size vagina. The rest of it can be determined standing."

Of course, her mother had been right. When she arrived at college, Kristen soon faced her mother's wisdom the hard way. San Diego colleges had a reputation for being party schools. Of course, one might conclude the same about any assemblage of young adults where the weather was warm enough to ensure students arrived to class in short shorts or tank tops most of the year. It hadn't taken Kristen many tries before discovering her personal Goldilocks fit.

Still, it thrilled her to come face to face with Tony's exceptional organ. Kristen accommodated him in every way she could, going out of her way to make their coupling work.

He had been gentle at first, no doubt sensitive to being too large for aggressive penetration. But when Kristen had slapped his face after he handled her breasts too hard, Tony's response had been one of excitement rather than calm, and he soon made her regret her action.

Kristen returned to bed and laid down only a moment before realizing her dog was no longer beside her. She realized Penelope hadn't been in bed when Kristen awoke, and she soon saw the bedroom door was open. A surge of adrenaline set her limbs on fire, and Kristen rose to make her way out the door, searching for her new pet.

Walking along the upstairs hall, Kristen called out to the animal with a sweet, high-pitched cooing, hoping to find all was okay. When Kristen arrived at the first landing of stairs, she saw Penelope dancing at the front door, wiggling her fluffy tail curl as if she were dying to be let out.

"Oh, what a sweet girl. Are you waiting for me?" Kristen asked, receiving a joyful panic from Penny's sweet face.

Kristen unlocked the door, and the dog bolted down the front porch steps to the grass beside them. Penelope let go of her burden with a soothing squat, and the animal's breathing slowed into relaxation.

"Good girl," said Kristen. "Go pee, that's a good girl."

Kristen strolled over to Penelope and stood nearby. When the dog had finished, Kristen again praised the animal and asked her to return to the house. Penelope walked right back in the front door, to Kristen's delight, instead of bolting away to reclaim her freedom.

"What a good girl!" cried Kristen as she climbed the steps behind her sweet, fluffy dog and shut the door behind them.

That was when Kristen's heart sank.

Looking at the downstairs living and dining rooms, the word 'disarray' didn't describe the scene before her. Had there been any furniture in the room, Kristen expected the resulting disaster might have been Biblical in nature. She seemed to have moved every single item in the room.

She'd overturned Tony's saw bench, its legs pointing in the air like a dead bug. Once stacked in perfect rows, she'd scattered Tony's finished wooden boards everywhere. Each board bore teeth marks as if they'd been nothing but giant chew toys to the dog. She had ripped the plastic wrapping off the uninstalled powder room sink and scattered it everywhere to fall like transparent autumn leaves. She'd clawed the closet door until she sanded its white paint off at the base.

How did a single bucket falling wake me, but I slept through all this?

Kristen heard a key slip into the front door lock. Tony appeared, carrying a large bag of dog food over his shoulder and a shopping bag filled with items in the other hand.

Entering the room, Tony stopped short as the door closed and let out a slow whistle, as if the scene impressed him as much as it shocked him. His eyes fell on Penelope, who sat several paces away near a wall. The dog shook as if she knew she was in trouble, but she was too excited to see him again to contain herself.

"No!" he shouted firmly at her, and the dog dropped her nose in deference and shame.

Tony dropped both bags onto the floor before stomping to the powder room door.

"Come here!" Tony demanded and pointed at the floor before him.

As if she were fighting against her own legs, Penelope maintained her posture, head lowered in shame.

"Inside," Tony commanded the animal.

Penelope lowered her head even deeper and moved into the small empty room.

Tony shut the powder room door just enough to make his point, soon eliciting a bevy of whimpers from the wretched animal.

He looked up at Kristen, who hadn't moved an inch since he arrived, and exhaled at length before touring the damage.

"I swear to god, I didn't let her out of the bedroom," Kristen promised. "The door was already open when I woke."

Tony exhaled at length once more.

"Clearly," he said.

Walking back to collect the shopping bag, he pulled out a thick round of cord before returning to the powder room with it. As he opened the door, Penelope stopped her whimpering and barked with joy to see Tony again.

"I know, sweetheart, I love you too," he said and knelt to say hello to the ecstatic pup. Tony then linked the cord to her collar and walked Penelope through the house and out the front door. Circling the residence, Tony brought Penelope to the backyard and tied the leash in an ideal spot so she could reach her bowl. With the extended leash, she could move around the garden without concern about her running off.

"It's enough to put her in there for a minute," Tony said when he returned, gesturing to the powder room. "Dogs hate isolation. Even for thirty seconds, shunning her is enough to make her sense she did something wrong. Penny's consequences don't need to be anything more than that for her to understand she's being punished."

Kristen heard Tony's words, but the enormity of everything that had happened weighed upon her.

"I guess I need to take her back," she said.

"What?" Tony scowled. "No, you can't do that now. Impounding a dog is the last choice. If Penny goes back there, they'll know the reason. Being aggressive with children is the only thing that sends a dog to the top of the kill list faster. They'll euthanize her within the week."

Kristen felt her wall crumbling, and her eyes became misty.

"Look, I'm sorry. I didn't mean to raise my voice," said Tony. "It'll all be fine. I'll show you how to take care of her. You just have to change your lifestyle a bit."

When Kristen didn't respond, Tony walked to the woman and put his arms around her.

"I'm sorry," he whispered.

Kristen felt herself fall into his comfort against her will. No one was more annoyed by her tears than she was. It annoyed Kristen to no end how she wept over the dumbest things imaginable. She had spent her career listening to real horrors, stories too dreadful to repeat even if they weren't confidential. Now she was sobbing like an idiot for needing dog care tips. Of course, it was more than that, but Tony's reminder of her idiocy had placed the metaphorical mirror in front of Kristen.

She pulled away from him, regaining her focus.

"Thank you, Tony," Kristen said, wiping her eyes. "I appreciate it. And you're right; I need to change my point of view."

"Why don't you take her for a jog? She needs all the exercise she can get, and you'll feel better, too."

Kristen nodded, her eyes observing the trashed floor.

"Tony, I'm sorry, but we can't do that again," she said without segue. "Last night wasn't fair to you, and nothing will come of it."

The young man furrowed his eyebrows. His observation of Kristen's declaration was silent.

"I won't lie and pretend I wasn't glad for it, but that isn't what I want our relationship to be about," Kristen continued. "So, I'll apologize again and ask that you oblige."

He looked down at the floor and scratched his face with the tops of his fingers.

"That's fine," Tony conceded. "Whatever you say."

"Thank you," Kristen offered. "Can I help you with all of this?"

"Don't worry about it," he shook his head. "Go take your jog. I'll handle this."

KRISTEN HAD JOGGED MORE IN THE PAST THREE DAYS than during the preceding three years. After her body had fallen to pieces on the third day, she discovered Penelope was the most unforgiving trainer in the world, pulling her new human's body up the Cambrian hills with little sympathy for splitting shins. The silver lining of Kristen's painful exertions was a Husky who slept like the dead throughout the night, cuddled up against her running partner in perfect bliss. Penelope was already asleep as Kristen combed through the ProQuest library search engine on her tablet, stretching out her last minutes of consciousness for the day.

Kristen browsed peer-reviewed "white papers" on paranormal psychology. Despite the stigma associated with the field, as it relied upon hypotheses that violated the core law of scientific research and discovery, Kristen found mountains of allegedly scholarly texts in every sub-genre.

Though Kristen would never admit it, she sought more evidence to support the experiences she'd discussed with her therapist. It was a method known as confirmation bias, a derided practice used by scientists who perform research and abandon any data that doesn't support the end conclusion they wish to prove true. Unfortunately, everyone is guilty regardless of whether they are conscious of their actions. As a therapist, Kristen reviewed herself and her patients with laser focus for any hint of confirmation bias, hoping to prevent it from leading to a misdiagnosis.

"If I'm to be fair to the process," Kristen whispered aloud, "I must research paranormal phenomena from the position that ghosts exist."

In many research publications, someone repeatedly quoted Joe Nickell as a source. Doctor Nickell was the author of several books on spirits, and some of his works focused on ghost sightings during the past two hundred years.

"Because all the accounts that come earlier are religious in nature," Kristen commented, unable to withhold a smirk.

Doctor Nickell had made a name for himself by exposing why hundreds of purported sightings or disturbances were hoaxes. His critics described him as 'a modern Sherlock Holmes.' He purportedly delineated why some ghosts haunted specific places while others haunted particular people.

The notion caught Kristen's attention.

She searched Nickell's work, finding publications on UFOs, conspiracy theories, and creatures like vampires, werewolves, and other monsters. To Kristen's disappointment, few of Nickell's books were downloadable. Pondering whether to order paperbacks and wait for them to arrive when she drove home in two days, she decided against pressing the button on the Amazon.com sales page.

"Yep, after researching a single thesis for four years, I'm now *that* person," Kristen whispered to her sleeping pup. "Instant gratification only, please."

Tired of reading but unwilling to give up consciousness,

Kristen turned to the podcast application on her iPad. More than a few came up on the search engine, but one stood out because of the cover art depicting two insane-looking women under the program title, *Wait, Whaaat?* Scanning through their episode titles and descriptions, Kristen surmised the talk show hosts were comedians. She selected an episode entitled *Don't Go Dumpster Diving for the Devil*, which promised a lengthy chat about ghosts.

"Perfect," said Kristen, and she closed her eyes.

The show's format was simple: two girlfriends, both high on overly-caffeinated beverages, chatted about whatever story they discovered that week on a paranormal subject. Naturally, the accounts didn't take up nearly as much of the program as their humorous commentary. The first story came from San Diego, which the hosts pointed out was officially the most haunted city in America.

Kristen remembered how the *Paranormal Activity* film series depicted a demon who appeared wherever the main protagonist lived.

"Well, that explains it," Kristen mused. "I must have brought the bastard to Cambria with me."

One host, Paula, recounted how a San Diego man woke up in the middle of the night to see his dead mother sitting in her dressing gown at the dining room table. The notion amused Kristen, but she would've been glad if her father appeared at the bathroom sink to brush his teeth.

The other host, Elaine, relayed how she experienced the ghost of her dead dog walking through her new home, one she purchased after the animal had died. She discussed the stamp of energy that some leave when they pass away. Sometimes the energy or spirit moves on, but sometimes it remains, or an imprint of them remains.

Kristen moved her hand to touch Penelope's white underbelly, feeling it rise and fall slowly.

The hosts then discussed the history of the Ouija board, from its creation during the Middle Ages to its eventual evolution into a parlor game in the 19th century. They reviewed how the spiritual beackon became a children's board game in the 20th century.

Kristen remembered how the little girl in *The Exorcist* opened the door to her infestation by communicating with her invisible friend through a Milton-Bradley Ouija board.

One man named Steve found a Latin Ouija board in a dumpster, and it spoke to him. He woke up at three-thirty in the morning to find his hand on the plastic indicator, which moved of its own accord. From the corner of the room, he heard a voice say, "Why are you hurting me?" The man quickly found Jesus and needed to read several Bible passages before he felt safe again.

"I don't know, Steve," said the podcast host, "you're just making bad decisions all around. I'm thinking Jesus would be like, 'First of all, you dug the Ouija board out of the trash and decided to play with it. So, frankly, we're done, dude. I have other things to worry about, like orphans in Calcutta.'"

They continued to describe a fifteen-year-old boy who played the game with his buddies one afternoon. That night, he woke up at three-fifteen and noticed a shadow on the wall of his darkened bedroom.

"What is it about that fucking hour?!" the host interrupted herself.

The boy couldn't understand how the shadow was being made, but after inspecting it, he returned to bed and found sleep. The boy continued to wake up all that week, shortly after three o'clock, to see more shadows on his bedroom walls. Finally, the boy awoke to his dog barking at the shadows as if they were all around them.

"See, and that's when you know you need to get the fuck out," the host said , evoking laughter from her partner.

Kristen smiled as she continued to feel her Husky's abdomen and its relaxed breathing that certified all was perfectly fine.

You just let me know, babe, Kristen thought in the moments before she, too, fell asleep.

CHAPTER TWENTY-ONE

At six minutes past three o'clock, Kristen's eyes opened to see shadows on the bedroom ceiling, cast by the bright moonlight pouring into the windows. She couldn't remember what she'd been dreaming about, but Kristen awoke to feel well-rested. At first, she didn't quite understand why her eyes had opened to darkness.

Reaching over to the bedside table, Kristen tapped to light the display of her smartwatch to read the time. From her periphery, she saw a dark shape on the room's far wall. Glancing and blinking to focus on the spot, Kristen saw that the tall black form was the bedroom doorway wide open to the darker hallway beyond.

A noise came from far away. It seemed like the sound of scraping.

Kristen sat up and realized her breathing in the silent room, still coming with the strong exhales of sleep.

Penelope was not in bed next to her. The dog's absence beside her affected Kristen more than she could process. Penelope was absent, and Kristen felt more alone than she ever had before the pup arrived.

"Penny!" Kristen's voice rose in the silence.

No response came but the light scraping sound from the hall.

Kristen pulled the covers away to release her legs from the bed. Consciousness was still a dull, intangible sensation as it attempted to take hold of her waking body. Kristen's feet hit the carpet below her bed, and she felt gravity balance her limbs in the darkness.

She was frightened, but Kristen was still too asleep to stop herself from stomping across the upstairs hallway. She moved to the stairs and held the railing to ensure her balance. Her feet met each step with concentration until she arrived at the ground floor.

"Penelope!" Kristen called, flipping the switch to light the downstairs wall lamps that released only a dull amber light through the protective paper Tony had wrapped them in.

From her right, Kristen heard the scratching sound from the coat closet in the living room. Its door hung wide open.

Walking around to stand before the door, Kristen squinted into the closet's dark. It extended back some eight feet under the decline of the stairwell. She switched the closet light on, but darkness remained. Kristen remembered Tony had damaged the lightbulb on his first day in the house.

She moved forward and crouched into the dark space, blinking to find the source of the sound. Penelope's feet tapped forward into the light to startle the woman.

"What are you doing?" Kristen whispered, as if to keep from waking up the empty house.

Penelope licked the woman's face before returning to the dark behind her, where the closet declined under the stairs to the left. Penelope let out a loud bark into the darkness, startling her human into stark focus.

"No!" answered Kristen, and she took Penelope by her

collar to walk her out of the small space before slamming the closet door behind them.

"Upstairs," she commanded.

The dog hesitated but followed her human as Kristen returned to the main bedroom. Kristen left on every light in the house. The thought of turning them off never entered her mind.

With the door closed behind them, Penelope made for the bed and circled half a dozen times before landing in the proper position to return to sleep.

"Just like that, huh?" Kristen muttered.

Though she was up early, Kristen was no longer tired, not enough to return to sleep. Her new running schedule, and the exhaustion it guaranteed, ensured she was white-knuckling consciousness by nine o'clock in the evening. The ensuing rest during the past few days had been akin to a miracle. Each morning had greeted Kristen with clarity, making coffee an unnecessary vice.

She took the small glass pot from the brewer to the faucet in the bathroom to fill it with two cups of water. When the machine was ready, she flipped the switch and waited for the first brew. Frankly, the fragrance was sufficient for Kristen, but she poured her first cup of Italian Roast and placed it on her bedside table. She fluffed the pillows to sit in bed, waiting for the coffee to cool to a drinkable temperature.

Opening the small bedside drawer, Kristen pulled out a folder of documents from her realtor. They included his preliminary pricing of the house based on his expectations of its value after Kristen completed the proposed renovations. Accompanying them was a layout of the projected state taxes and fees for his services.

Kristen found notes about prior owners on the last page. The lot had first been purchased in 1977 by Thomas William.

The house he built was transferred to his son, Valon William, the following year as an inheritance.

Under these bullets was information the realtor highlighted in yellow with a written note: 'Must disclose to potential buyers.' The son had died in 1984 because of homicide, and his murder had occurred on the property.

"What the hell?" remarked Kristen with a quick scowl.

Penelope's eyes opened, and she lifted her head to attend to her human's raised voice.

Kristen reached to touch the animal, who returned her head to the sheets in moments.

The remaining bullets showed the house went to local state ownership and was sold at auction in 1992 to Pamela Hill. The house was last sold last to Henry and Margaret Cole in 2015.

CHAPTER TWENTY-TWO

Penelope ran to Tony when he arrived that morning, leaping as if they hadn't seen each other in years. She provided him with the requisite wet kisses. Arriving on the first floor for her morning run, Kristen gave Tony little more than a cordial salutation.

He should be grateful that nothing had changed between them after the other day. Tony had expected Kristen to fire him when he walked upstairs to continue the argument she tried to end. The sex had been intense, or at least Tony had thought so. The two seemed to understand what they needed from each other. And when it was over, Kristen seemed satisfied and glad.

However, the next morning, she stopped their affair before it could go anywhere further. Theirs would be a professional relationship, Kristen declared, and nothing else. Tony had agreed to her declaration because there wasn't much else for him to say. It was Kristen's house, and he was her employee. She didn't have trouble attracting suitors, so what else could he do without crossing the line? The flavor of defeatism burned like cinders in Tony's mouth.

Just after ten o'clock, Kristen returned from her morning run with Penelope, who shot up to Tony in the driveway to say hello again.

"How did she do?"

"She's doing great," Kristen answered, with heavy panting. "I'm the one who's making a puddle."

California's early autumn heat had broken for a couple of days, but it returned with a vengeance this morning. A sopping sheen of perspiration covered every square inch of Kristen's exposed skin.

"Don't think Penny doesn't feel it, too, with that coat of hers," Tony replied. "Make sure she has fresh water."

"On my way," said Kristen, a hint of annoyance in her voice.

Tony hadn't meant to sound as if he were chastising her. In the past four days, she'd more than proven herself cut out to be a fit guardian for Penny. Nevertheless, he didn't comment further to correct the impression but let them go ahead to the backyard.

At a distance, Tony noticed a black sports car pull up to the curb in front of the house. Kristen hadn't advised Tony to expect Ryan was visiting her this morning. From what he could tell, Tony assumed Kristen did not know the man was coming over, considering her stinking, drenched state. Then again, maybe the guy liked that.

Ryan soon made his way up the hill to the house, holding an arrangement of red roses. Arriving at the front porch, Ryan gave Tony a smile and a nod.

"She's back there," said Tony before the man could ring the doorbell, and he nodded to the gate at the end of the driveway leading to the rear yard.

Ryan thanked him and strolled around the house past Tony to find the object of his affection. The man wore a simple navy button-down shirt tucked into well-cut silk charcoal pants with fine leather shoes.

As unimpressed as Tony liked to think he was with the guy, he couldn't help but notice how well-dressed the man appeared, even in simple clothing. When Ryan pulled on the door, Penny fired off a ferocious round of barking at the intruder. Tony couldn't help but smile.

Their conversation improved after Kristen had gotten the dog to calm down and let Ryan introduce himself to the suspicious animal. Indeed, he had come unannounced and uninvited. It was a questionable move, but it seemed to be one Ryan thought would work. Tony couldn't help but listen to the exchange at first, but the bitter adrenaline flooding his system soon caused the young man to walk back inside the house.

In time, Kristen popped inside and stole upstairs with her new flowers. Looking through the rear glass door, Tony saw Ryan stay in the backyard, where he'd taken a seat and petted Penny. The man was waiting for Kristen to change to go out with him.

Tony felt stupid about his reaction. Despite how he felt about the matter, Tony was not in a relationship with Kristen. There was also no logical reason to despise someone for petting a dog Tony didn't even own. Yet, with both truths in front of him, the young man couldn't help but feel the sickening sting of jealousy. Tony did his best to focus on the day's work, soon needing to turn up the volume on his headphones to drown out his seething thoughts.

Half an hour passed while track after track of Parkway Drive's rage metal blared in Tony's ears. The band's aggressive sound finally drove an idea into his mind, and Tony walked outside to make it happen.

Arriving at his truck, Tony removed his headphones and

lowered the tailgate to sit on it. He pulled out his Thermos lunch box and set it beside himself. Tony then slipped off his shirt, letting the late morning sun beat down on his muscled back and ink. A minute passed before he heard the home's back door open. Kristen announced to Ryan she was ready. Tony heard the pair exit the rear gate and walk down the driveway behind him. When they arrived at the end of his truck, Tony's idea paid off as planned.

Kristen stared at the young man with undisguised irritation in her eyes. She couldn't speak for at least four seconds as she and Ryan stared at Tony's half-naked physique and the turkey sandwich held to his mouth.

"Ryan and I are heading out," Kristen said with a slight sound of resentment in her voice. "We'll be back in a few hours."

With that, she turned, and they walked away down the hill toward Ryan's car.

Tony didn't bother to look at Ryan as they left but unashamedly stared at Kristen's ass as she moved off, in case the man might turn back and notice.

With a phony demeanor, Kristen shot around and hollered to Tony.

"If I decide not to come home before you leave, I'll call you to let you know," she said with a broad grin.

Tony responded with animated nods and a deep frown of understanding, holding his right hand to his head in the symbol of a telephone receiver.

Touché, he thought.

CHAPTER TWENTY-THREE

RYAN HAD DRIVEN THEM UP THE COAST TO Leffingwell Landing, a picturesque preserve surrounded by gentle hills and stately pine trees at the foot of the Pacific break. Ryan found them a shaded wooden picnic table on lush green grass along the cliffside, where the surf pounded against the rocks. He also brought a picnic basket for lunch, a treat filled with cheese, meats, sandwiches, and a cold bottle of Sauvignon Blanc.

It was the type of date Kristen had dreamt of as a girl, inspired by some Nora Roberts romance novel her mother had left around their home. Ryan again created intimacy in a very public place, offering the couple another opportunity to relax and become familiar with one another.

But Kristen couldn't relax. Her anger at Tony clouded her every thought.

"I'm sorry if I'm quiet," she apologized to Ryan. "I've had a lot on my mind, and this is such a lovely spot."

"You're not the first only child I've known," he smiled.

"I'm glad because the conversation department requires a lot of work. We don't seem quite to notice when the discussion stops. I've had to clarify with many friends that I'm not quiet because I'm upset with them."

"Oh, I get it. I have to steer the ship," Ryan laughed. "Tell me about Penelope."

"I have the sweetest dog in the world," Kristen answered. "We were meant to be together. I realize how that sounds, but I'm convinced of it. We've taken to each other so well; I wish I'd brought her here. She'd love this place. Penelope loves anywhere she can run about and play."

"And she's quite the fan of attention, I can confirm," Ryan said. "Insatiable, more like it. She couldn't get enough of the head massage I gave her. You said you adopted her in San Luis Obispo?"

"I did," Kristen nodded. "During my career, I've recommended to at least a hundred patients suffering from any ailment you can think of that they ought to find a pet to keep their minds and bodies active. I took my advice and found the closest shelter. When I got there, I told the lady helping me how I was looking for a young dog that liked to exercise on account of my needing to get back into jogging. No sooner had I said it than we turned a corner, and there Penelope was, ready to go. It was as if she had been waiting for me. The shelter attendant kept asking me to look at the other dogs, but Penelope and I couldn't take our eyes off each other."

"A dream come true for both of you," he declared. "And she likes to run?"

"Far more than I ever will," Kristen giggled. "Every step is an adventure to her, and she makes me go further than I ever would without her."

"Well, it's truly a romance then," his eyes sharpened at the corners.

Ryan lifted his glass to invite a clink from Kristen, who was only too happy to toast to the occasion.

"So, how do I get you to change your mind about leaving town tomorrow?" he asked, leaning forward to draw her attention.

Kristen gave him a coy smile and reached to pull her red hair behind her ear as the ocean breeze picked up.

"Well, there it is," he added, raising his hands with a plea for mercy. "How will you fall in love with me from three hundred miles away?"

"We're going to have to do our best," she answered, raising her eyebrows. "My work is there; my life is there. I'm not opposed to moving one day, but I'll be hard-pressed to find a better place to live. I can't wait to see the look on Penelope's face when she gets a load of the places I'm going to take her to run."

"I'm sure you'll be happy together," he quipped.

"I'm serious. How else can this happen if you don't come down to me? The entire purpose of hiring an overseer to manage the renovations on the house was because I can't stay here to do it myself."

"I know," he jutted his chin and ran his hand through a gold lock that fell forward in the breeze. "So, we have to make this work on the weekends?"

"My schedule at the hospital changes all the time. Sometimes I work on the weekends, but I'll have Monday and Tuesday off some weeks. In other months, it'll be Tuesday and Thursday. It all depends on what's needed."

Ryan nodded in appreciation of the feat she laid before him.

"Well, to be clear, I mean to make this happen. I understand the obstacles, but there's no way I'll let you slip away without a fight."

Kristen took another swallow of the cold wine. As difficult as it was for her to imagine how a long-distance arrangement was workable, it felt good to hear someone say such a thing to her.

"All right, then," Kristen answered, "let's try it."

The woman promised to give Ryan her schedule when she returned home and had enough time to re-acclimate herself to work. There was something comforting about how this man seemed to feel about Kristen.

When they'd finished lunch, Ryan offered to take Kristen on a walk, but she declined because of her legs, almost dead from the morning run, though the wine had dulled their fatigue.

Upon returning home just after three o'clock, Ryan walked Kristen to her door. With Tony still on the premises, she understood Ryan wouldn't want to come in. Frankly, Kristen was glad of it. Just seeing Tony's truck in the driveway brought her agitation to the surface again. When Ryan had kissed her goodbye, Kristen first went around the house to check in on Penelope and let her know she'd returned.

"Had a good time?" Tony asked without an attitude when Kristen returned to the house.

The young man's shirt was back on, but it now was a tank top with some graphic of a gym printed on the back.

"You and I had an agreement," Kristen said to Tony instead of a response.

"We have an agreement, don't we?" he replied. "At least a couple, if I understand you."

"We agreed about the dress code. Don't bother explaining yourself," said Kristen, holding up her hand to stop his response. "I know what you were doing. It was unprofessional, and I didn't appreciate it."

"I was on my lunch break, and it's pretty warm," he started.

"That's bullshit, Tony," she cut him off. "I told you there couldn't be anything more between us. I don't need you flaunting like a child to get a rise out of the men I date."

"Did it? Did it get a rise out of your friend?" he asked boldly, a smile breaking on his face. "You're home a lot earlier than I expected. I guess he had little to offer."

Kristen released an incredulous laugh.

"I can't believe you," she shook her head. "How insecure could you be?

"What do I have to be insecure about?" he challenged her.

"Enough, Tony," she walked up to him. "I need you to be more professional, that's all."

"No, by all means," he continued, "please, tell me why I'm insecure, Doctor."

"For starters, you're a kid," she answered, despite her intentions. "One who lives in a party van."

"I live how I want to," he replied, still unfazed by Kristen's taunts.

"Fine, but I don't have to guess how it goes over with the women you date."

"Haven't had any complaints."

"Oh?" she eyed him with mock suspicion. "How kind of them to spare your feelings. Then let me be the first woman to be honest with you. No one is interested in a back-alley date with Shaggy in his Mystery Machine."

Tony laughed despite himself.

"They don't have any trouble finding their way back to beg for more," he replied.

Kristen exhaled, at once upset with herself for drawing the argument out. She didn't want to deal with it any longer. She would be gone in the morning and done with him.

"Can you just stop?" Kristen asked with impatience seizing her frame. "Am I asking too much that you just stop with all this nonsense? He has nothing to do with you."

"I'm not sure what you want me to do," Tony answered, raising his arms to place his hands behind his head. "You're leaving tomorrow, so what difference does it make? Unless you plan on coming back every weekend to sniff some Tesla dick out."

Kristen's hand flew out at Tony's face and slapped him. The sound of her palm landing on the young man's face shocked her as much as it doubtless affected him. Kristen couldn't believe what Tony had said, or that she'd unraveled so far out of control as to strike him.

Tony clearly hadn't expected it, but he smiled all the same.

He stepped closer to her, far too close for Kristen's comfort, though he didn't intimidate her. She could smell him now, and Kristen's eyes averted to hide her desire for him to touch her, finding their way to anything else. She stared at Tony's tattoo of the Vitruvian Man on his hard shoulder, and she felt his warm breath on her neck as he pulled Kristen closer to have her.

CHAPTER TWENTY-FOUR

WHEN THEY HAD BOTH EXHAUSTED THEMSELVES, THEY discussed nothing more. The first acts of their behavior had begun on the ground level, requiring a flustered search for any bit of empty wall to rely on for support. Then it became the staircase that allowed her to open to him. Afterward, they went to her bed to finish their marathon and recover. The room stifling from the afternoon heat, insisting their perspiration wouldn't cool down their bodies. In time, Tony rose, found whatever clothes lay about, dressed as much as he could, and returned downstairs to locate his shirt and prepare to leave for the day.

It alarmed Kristen how focused and clear her mind became after sex. The anger and frustration that had barked at Tony earlier vanished in the afterglow, as had her deep concern for the proprieties of their working relationship. Its absence now showed Kristen how her once logical conclusions were nothing more than counterfeit reasons to keep the young man out of her bed. Indeed, Tony was a complication, but one she might need. Still, Kristen would rarely see him once she left for home, and their future exchanges would be over the telephone until she returned in a few months to inspect the work.

Kristen would leave at seven o'clock tomorrow evening, which allowed her twenty-four hours to finish packing. Lists ran through her mind about what she had to do before returning to San Diego. Ryan's unplanned outing had thrown her schedule off, and she would need to rally the rest of her time to complete everything that needed doing. The boxes filled with her parent's belongings had been reviewed, donated, or taped up for shipping. Kristen would need to label the boxes for the shipping truck to collect them tomorrow afternoon.

The woman had already installed Penelope's safety harness in the back seat of her car. Kristen had also packed food and water and scouted out a few potential sites from her phone browser for when the Husky needed a break from the vehicle. Tony had promised the animal would settle down after a few minutes of driving if Kristen played calm music or an audiobook. She created a playlist on her phone to stream for the Husky, and she had a Dan Brown thriller ready to keep her eyes awake. With luck, the dog would go to sleep once the dark of night arrived.

Kristen's telephone buzzed, and she turned to find the home renovation designer calling.

"Hello, this is Kristen Cole," she answered.

"Good afternoon, Miss Cole. Harrold Lankershim calling from Synergize Home Design. How are you?"

"I'm doing well. What's up?" Kristen answered, standing up to close her bedroom door.

"I'm calling to discuss the reports I've received from the contractors I have performing your renovation work," Lankershim began, his gruff voice resonating through the telephone. "I've heard from a few men now that they're unhappy about how your site manager handles them."

"What do you mean?" Kristen asked, just as calmly.

"I'm told he's been offering... feedback, shall we say," the man continued, "and it's rubbing them the wrong way. Now, I've heard these reports from two separate individuals who don't know each other and haven't worked there at the same time. So, I'm taking what they've reported seriously."

"Of course," Kristen responded. "Go on."

"The electrician I sent to inspect your wiring told me your man criticized his work," continued Lankershim. "First, it was a problem when he arrived a few minutes late, but then issues got pointed out to the man about how he does his job. None of those comments sat well with him.

"The second person—he's an acoustical carpenter— arrived at another time to do the dry-walling. He claims your man asked a dozen tiresome questions about his methods and why he was doing this or that. Then, your guy criticized him for not sweeping up when he wanted it swept. Tony, I believe his name is, chastised the guy for... cleanliness... and swept up after the drywaller before he'd even finished for the day."

Kristen heard Lankershim's voice rise as if the discussion were agitating him.

"Normally, I would handle this matter myself," he continued, "but as I haven't hired him, I need you to handle this."

"That's reasonable," Kristin confirmed. "As it happens, I was present when those incidents took place. Frankly, I'm surprised that either man would have anything to tell you about Tony."

Kristen allowed Lankershim a moment to respond, but he remained silent.

"First," she began, "the electrician didn't arrive a few minutes late—he arrived hours late. He was a no-show. Tony called the number you provided in your schedule, and the man never answered by voice or text. Your man didn't give us a peep until he showed up unannounced later in the afternoon. He had difficulty apologizing for wasting my time and money when he arrived. But no one's perfect, and I need the work completed, so I asked Tony to give him another shot.

"Second," she continued, "even if the man didn't care to field questions about his work, it amazes me he would have the nerve to complain about discussing the details of his service with his site manager. His job affects everyone else's—a job he's shown so little concern for.

"I can say the same for the drywaller," continued Kristen, "who assured Tony he'd leave the site clean after leaving his garbage all over my house on his first day. That request came from me. I narrowly avoided tripping over broken and unused pieces he left in the way. I told the man he needed to understand people were living in this work site and to please respect my need for safety. Your man couldn't keep his mess off the walking paths even after that conversation. Instead, he left an unnecessary hazard in every room. Tony did the man a favor by cleaning up after him. But instead of expressing gratitude, he's bothering you with grievances.

"But again," she repeated herself, "why he should be uncomfortable explaining the protocols of his job function to his site manager is beyond me."

Lankershim wasn't quick to respond, but a dark agitation lowered his voice when he returned.

"Yes, your name came up in both conversations," he responded. "I don't work like this. When we design a job, we install our site manager to ensure they perform the work to our standards. Now, we made an exception for you because of your timetable. But I will not place my work relationships at risk…"

"You've got to be kidding me," Kristen interrupted Lankershim. "So, you're saying you're fine with those contractors' performance and have an issue with me speaking to them when they fail?"

"Miss, a construction site differs from wherever you're accustomed to. My contractors work in many sites we oversee, and we haven't had these problems with them in the past."

"I find that difficult to believe," Kristen answered, her voice calm, "considering how mediocre their performance was in my house. Perhaps that's what you're trying to tell me, that I'm expecting too much?"

"We have the highest expectations from our subcontractors, and we guarantee the quality of work they perform," he countered. "The matter here is that these men work for me, and I work for you. Now, if there's an issue you'd like to address, I should be the one to approach them."

"I see," said Kristen, "and by your admission, you disagree with my expectations of your men's performance."

"I have been in this business a very—

"No, that's fine. If this arrangement doesn't work for you, I won't ask you to make concessions. I understand we need to go our separate ways."

"Ma'am, that isn't what I'm saying—

"You've made your position crystal clear, Harold," the psychologist interrupted him again. "I will use someone else to complete this job."

"We have a contract—

"And you've told me you're not willing or able to do the work under the agreed-upon conditions," Kristen cut him off a third time. "Unless you mean to say that another site manager of your choice will arrive in the morning to take over for the duration of the job, it seems clear to me you've backed out of the contract. I'm saying to you I understand your position, disagree with the new terms you wish to impose, and agree our contract is void. You may return my deposit by check, minus the administration fees outlined in the contract, within sixty days. Is there anything else?"

Lankershim didn't respond.

"No? Very well, then. My best to you, and good afternoon," Kristen said, closing the line.

Even more shocking to Kristen than her response was that she hadn't felt the slightest pang of adrenaline until after she'd closed the line. Then a flood of the fiery hormone rushed through her limbs, forcing her to pace about the room.

Kristen hadn't even negotiated with the man to arrive at another resolution. Instead, she'd pushed the disagreement to end with separation. Now, she'd need to change everything else to accommodate the consequences of her action, and her options were few.

Kristen searched for Tony downstairs, finding him in the driveway, where he was closing his vehicle to leave for the day.

"We need to talk."

Tony couldn't stop his eyes from squinting at her words, and Kristen realized he must be anticipating another discussion about their professional relationship.

"I've just gotten off the phone with the design firm," she began, "and it seems they'll no longer be working with us."

"What do you mean?" Tony scowled in surprise.

"It's a long story," she continued, "but I must find another company to do the work. So, I'll need to stay until I find them. It's late, but I'll start making phone calls and leaving requests for bids. When I started, one other company seemed like they could do the work for a higher price, so I'll call them too and see what the options are."

Tony lowered his gaze, pondering her announcement.

"What?" she smiled. "Did you think I would tell you to be more professional at work? Fine. If you wouldn't mind, could you be more professional when we're not in bed?"

Kristen smirked and rolled her eyes before returning to the front door.

"Wait a minute," Tony called.

CHAPTER TWENTY-FIVE

IT WAS THE DREAM WITH RYAN AGAIN, JUST AS IT HAD come to Kristen on earlier nights. Again, Ryan took her with all his greedy invasions, delighting Kristen with how much he loved coupling with her. When he penetrated her, she soon felt the release she'd craved. In time, Ryan brought himself on top of her, nuzzling her ear and nibbling with each deep thrust. But as Kristen turned to kiss him, Ryan licked her face. His tongue came with deep, wet pulls all over her cheeks. Ryan even licked at her eyelids, to her profound confusion.

Opening her eyes, Kristen found Penelope's sweet eyes staring at her. It was the third morning in a row that Kristen had enjoyed the same dream, devoid of the horrors she first experienced. As each played out, Penelope's wet kisses had woken her. It was time for both ladies to relieve themselves.

"Okay, I'm getting up," Kristen moaned.

Penelope sat back in delighted triumph, then hopped down to stand before the bedroom door, waiting for Kristen to drag herself first to the bathroom. In moments, the dog led the way to the front door to be let onto the grass, where relief came.

"Breakfast," Kristen said with her best imitation of high-pitched excitement. The pair made their way to the backyard, where Penelope displayed her obvious joy at finding her water dish and circling with delight when Kristen dug into the food bag to fill her bowl.

Kristen attached the extended leash to Penelope's collar while she ate greedily. She heard Tony's work truck arriving up the driveway and returned to the front to greet him.

The past three days had brought with it an unexpected change in Tony. Since convincing Kristen he could handle the renovation by himself, including hiring professionals and designing the remodel, she had noticed an obvious change in him. He'd become invested in the project like never before. A sense of focused, disciplined urgency moved his mind throughout the day. For example, when the new carpenter arrived yesterday morning to measure the kitchen for cabinetry. Tony invested his entire day with the man, communicating his goals, offering to assist in any way needed, praising the day's work, and developing a mutual respect that brought the best out of both men.

Kristen had extended her stay. The hospital allowed her to dip into her sick pay because her bereavement time had run out. She wouldn't get more than another week without facing severe problems, but after three days, Kristen felt confident she could leave anytime. Tony had proven himself to be her savior. He hadn't intimated wanting to take Kristen to bed during the transition. It was as if that part of him only made itself known when the two argued. Considering the quality of his work, Kristen might have to make something up to complain about if she hoped for any more action.

"Morning," Tony said, bright-eyed and happy to be there.

"Good morning," she answered. "I just took Penelope out for her breakfast."

"I stopped by the cafe to pick us up something," he said, lifting a carrier with two coffees and a small paper bag of baked goods.

"Read my mind," Kristen responded with delight.

The two sat on the small sofa on the house's front porch, the dark wood covered by dark navy cushions. Tony handed Kristen her drink and three packets of brown sugar. When she'd stirred the poison in, he handed her a chocolate muffin, which Kristen received with all the wonderment of a deprived child.

"Oh, wow. Thank you," she cried with glee.

"They hadn't even made it into the display window yet," Tony commented as he pulled the white wax paper from the edge of his still-warm muffin.

"Heaven," she sighed as the chocolate sprayed her brain with dopamine. "So, what's your plan for the day?"

"I have an electrician coming to review and prepare plans for ceiling lighting on both floors. I'll be working to repair the wainscoting in the living room."

"I'm thinking you have this all under control. Am I correct?"

"I believe so," he answered.

"Then I'm going to leave for home tonight. Is that cool?"

Tony nodded without emotion. "That should be fine."

"Okay," she answered with relief, "I think I have everything ready, more or less. I'll reschedule the movers for their next available time and message you with the information if I don't get it completed by tonight. I'll leave my bedroom otherwise empty, and you can cover the bed and side tables with a tarp whenever you get around to painting in there."

"Sounds good," Tony agreed.

"Thank you again," Kristen placed her hand on his forearm. "I could never have done this all without your help. I can't wait to see what you do with it. If there's anything you need, please let me know. I'm here for you, okay?"

"Thank you," he answered with appreciation. "I'm grateful for the opportunity."

They sat in silence, enjoying the morning breeze that promised a much cooler day than the past week had offered. When Kristen finished her muffin, she placed her garbage in the small paper bag and rose from the sofa.

"I'm going to start my day," she said, returning to her bedroom to shower.

By ten o'clock, she had dressed and packed for her evening departure. Kristen would wait until four o'clock to run Penelope, which would hopefully tire her out and make sure she slept for most of the five-hour drive to San Diego.

Before Kristen stripped the bed, she heard the doorbell ring. Making her way downstairs, she saw Ryan through the glass sidelight as he stood outside the front door.

What's he doing here? she wondered. Kristen had spoken to Ryan several times in the past days, relaying the events that had kept her in Cambria, but she had been clear she was busy, only staying behind to attend to business.

"You're unexpected," said Kristen, opening the front door.

"Good morning," said Ryan, leaning in to give her a warm kiss on the cheek.

"What's up?" Kristen asked, keeping her impatience behind her smile.

"I hear everything is going well for you. I take it we averted the crisis?"

"Yes, it's all worked out pretty well. I was getting ready to head for home."

"Well, I'm glad to catch you before you head out. What do you say to a little time together before you leave?"

It wasn't something Kristen wanted, but she couldn't help but feel gratified he had thought of her in this way.

"Ah..." Kristen hesitated. "I've still got much to do before I can leave."

"I won't fly you anywhere you need a passport for," Ryan answered with a light smirk, "just a quick drive and a little bite to eat? Didn't you say you prefer to drive through L.A. after the evening traffic dies down?"

"Yeah, okay," answered Kristen with reluctance, "That sounds fine. Let me go get ready."

"You look perfect," he said. "There's no need to change, I promise."

"Fine, let me just get my bag. I'll be down in a minute."

Kristen left Ryan at the front door, motioning him to step inside, then stole away upstairs. She wasn't stepping out on a date without makeup or a better top, no matter what false flattery the man used.

When she returned downstairs, the front door was closed, and she saw the back of Ryan's head through the living room window as he sat on the porch sofa. Inside, Tony worked on the wainscoting.

"I'm stepping out for lunch," Kristen said to Tony. "I'll be back soon. Message me if you need anything."

"Will do," he said, glancing at her for a second to confirm.

"Thanks," Kristen said, aware of the man's change in attitude.

Yeah, well, that's the way love goes, she thought before finding her way onto the porch to head out with Ryan.

RYAN DROVE THEM UP HIGHWAY 45, EAST TOWARDS Paso Robles. The oak passage had just turned toward Autumn, and the vineyards were busy as farmers brought their summer growth to a close. The long-awaited break in the late summer heat meant the vintners were again racing to unburden their vines of the year's grapes before the last growths spoiled.

Kristen knew little about wine besides how to drink it, a behavior that hadn't required extensive education. She had admitted to Ryan on their earlier date he couldn't go wrong with a bottle of wine and a cheese board if he meant to treat her to a good time. And he'd heard every word of Kristen's proclamation.

Turning off the highway onto Vineyard Way, he jetted up the road in his Tesla, taking her mind off the journey as best he could with talk of his work and opinions on politics and art. At one point, he turned the car into a simple driveway that stopped at a massive, dark red iron gate. A stone wall adorned with the name 'Denner' flanked the impressive installation.

"You know where you're going?" Kristen asked, revealing a tremor of concern.

Ryan lowered his driver's window to an outstretched iron arm that held a keypad, into which he typed in a numerical code. The massive steel gates opened inward, clearing the road for them to proceed. Kristen guessed Ryan didn't live on this estate, but it was obvious he wasn't a stranger.

Pulling the black Tesla forward through a winding road of ripened vineyards on either side, Ryan found his way to a small parking lot beside a complex of modern mustard-colored buildings with dark metallic roofs that sloped this way and that. At one end of the complex, massive burned-red steel girders swept out from the roof, offering shade to a smattering of elegant wooden tables on the patio.

The seating areas around the building accommodated large parties. Their size was even more impressive because they were empty at present. Arriving at the front door, Ryan nodded to their right, where the outdoor spaces started.

"Head over that way and find a place you'd like to sit," Ryan instructed her. "I'm going to head inside and tell them we're here, okay?"

"You're sure?" Kristen asked, uncertain if she should take the liberty. The absence of other people made it feel like they were trespassing in someone's home.

"Oh, yes, they're expecting us," he said. "We can sit wherever we like."

Kristen stepped away as Ryan pulled the broad door of burned iron and glass to enter the winery, finding a small path leading her to the complex's western side. She moved through various areas—some expansive, some small and private—and arrived under an outcrop of monstrous oak trees that overlooked a manicured garden. Beneath wise old trees were areas designed to host special events. Near the end of a small lawn was a clearing designed to accommodate weddings or other once-in-a-lifetime moments.

Kristen envisioned white folding seats on either side of the path to accommodate wedding guests.

Kristen found an oval clearing under the largest tree. Beyond lovely, she imagined someone might officiate her wedding there. However, three elegant wooden tables with chairs filled the space today, so Kristen pulled a seat and established herself at the center table.

In the distance was a breathtaking vista of dark green vines growing over the lazy nearby hills. A bit of heaven was realized here, and the light breeze moved over the patch to ensure Kristen's comfort.

In time, Ryan appeared carrying an uncorked bottle of rosé in a small steel bucket of ice with two glasses. His blond hair gleamed like gold in the midday light, even now with its shorter cut.

"Beautiful, isn't this?" he said, placing the glasses on the small table and pouring the wine for them both before seating.

"I've been wine tasting in the area before," Kristen acknowledged, "but I've seen nothing like this."

"You need to let me show you around the neighborhood. There are so many wonderful estates here. But this one is pretty special. Look at this view," Ryan sighed with satisfaction, finding his seat.

"I'd guess they must do a lot of weddings right here," Kristen said.

"Something to think about," Ryan winked.

Kristen smiled at the comment. It would be unlike her to let that type of statement fly by if a patient had offered it during a session. Considering how it triggered her, Kristen had little choice but to push through her intimidation.

"Are you ready to discuss marriage?" she asked, amused by her nerve.

"It wasn't a subject ever on my mind before I met you," Ryan answered, his face an unexpected vision of sincerity.

Kristen was more unprepared for his response than she'd been for his teasing wink. The intimidation caused her to lower her gaze to the pink wine, shimmering like a jewel in the glass.

"You've known me for... has it been a week?" Kristen asked in an incredulous shake of her head.

"Almost three," he corrected her flippant remark. "How about that? That's got to mean something, doesn't it? I went thirty-six years tolerating only the vaguest acknowledgment that marriage exists. Then you arrive in my life, and it's become something I think of every day. What's that all about?"

Kristen moved forward in her seat as if to respond, but the words got stuck in her throat, and she exhaled instead. She reached for her glass and took a long drink.

A middle-aged man in a white polo shirt and plaid shorts arrived at their table with a large wooden platter of cheeses and charcuterie. The man looked like he lived there and had just been lounging at home, watching television. He laid the board between them and, after rushing through the various offerings, excused himself to return to the main building.

Kristen and Ryan filled the silence between them by reaching for something off the plate, following their selected morsel with a sip of the delicious, light wine.

"Everything about you just fits," Ryan said in time. "You're a beautiful woman and incredibly sexy, but you're not the only one I've ever encountered. It's... everything else. Where you're from, how you got there, and what you accomplished with what life gave you. Please don't be weirded out that I love hearing your father's voice when you comment on something as he would. It's so much more than that. You're clever and blunt; you make no room for pretense—

"No, that's a curse," she cut him off with a smile. "I'd give anything to keep from telling people how stupid they are."

"You're also savagely funny, especially when you've had some wine," Ryan acknowledged, reaching to lift the bottle and replace the missing drink in Kristen's glass. "I don't have room for people who can't make me laugh."

Kristen frowned her face for a moment, then shook the sentiment away.

"Two years," she said firmly. "That's how long it takes for all this excitement we're going through to wear off."

"What do you mean? What are we going through?" Ryan raised his eyebrow.

"Infatuation," she answered him. "These feelings where we think everything is diamonds and rosé." Kristen lifted her glass to take another drink of the crisp wine.

"Is that what this is?" he squinted. "Infatuation? I feel rather level-headed about it. I don't think of you like a new toy I'll be done with after an hour. Or in two years, as you say."

"You don't know who I am yet," Kristen implored him, pulling her red hair behind her ear. A poker player would call it a *tell*. "All you've seen is Magic Kristen, the woman who appears on dates with her hair flat-ironed and dances under the fireworks at fairytale castles. That represents maybe one percent of what you're getting yourself into with me."

"I've seen far more than Magic Kristen," he insisted. "I've seen Annoyed Kristen, Impatient Kristen, Unprepared Kristen, and Wounded Kristen. Which ones have I missed?"

She made to answer him, but Ryan held up his hand.

"No, don't tell me. I don't want any spoilers. I want to meet her for real."

"You haven't even slept with me," she said with uncharacteristic aplomb, "and to the point, you've had ample opportunity, with your goddamn romantic lips and smelling so good."

"That's fair," he nodded. "So, what are you doing later?"

Kristen laughed and sat back in her seat, exhausted by the conversation.

"I'm driving five to seven hours through the bowels of Hell to go home," she said, looking off at the view in frustration.

"No, you're not," said Ryan. "To hell with that."

CHAPTER TWENTY-SEVEN

TONY HAD FELT OVERJOYED DURING THE PAST THREE days. Kristen's decision to let him take complete charge of the renovations had given the man an even greater sense of drive, and so far, everything had gone better than he'd hoped. Tony was working toward something he wanted, which had arrived via a method he hadn't foreseen. His expanded vision of himself had brought a thrilling sense of accomplishment and seen the days fly faster than he could accept.

That was until this morning, when the black Tesla returned to the house.

Tony had agreed his relationship with Kristen should remain professional, but things had changed when she'd taken him to her bed the second time. Or so he thought. Watching Kristen receive Ryan and leave on a date this morning had wounded Tony more than he could've foreseen. He didn't want to acknowledge it, but watching her bid him a casual goodbye as if it were nothing had enraged the young man. It took all his self-discipline to keep from punching a hole through the drywall.

But as much as Tony hated it, he understood why Kristen

hadn't thought twice about accepting Ryan's offer. Tony was just a fuck—a means to an end for Kristen, and her older suitor offered the woman something far more. Ryan had commonalities with Kristen: he was an intellectual and well-accomplished in his career. Driving that hundred-thousand-dollar sports car was indicator enough, even if Tony didn't know what the man had done to obtain it.

When the afternoon continued without a sign of Kristen, Tony presumed he might not see her before packing up this evening to drive home. He pondered if he should message her to verify, but he couldn't bring himself to type the question into his cell phone. While considering the action, Tony's phone vibrated, and Kristen's name appeared on the screen.

"Hello?" he answered.

"Hey, Tony, this is Kristen," she said far too loudly, as if she were drunk.

"Hey there, boss," he said without emotion.

"Listen," she continued, "I'm not returning before you shut down for the day. I've postponed my drive home, at least until tomorrow. When you lock up, would you leave the lights on for me and ensure that Penelope has water? I'll feed her when I get home."

"Sure, you got it. I'll be heading out in thirty minutes, and I'll make sure everything's covered."

"You're awesome! I'll see you tomorrow," Kristen said, giggling as she attempted in vain to close the phone line for several seconds.

The sound was a knife in Tony's gut. He thought about chucking the cell phone through the window, picturing the shattered glass falling over the front porch. The image played over and over in Tony's mind. He saw the event from multiple angles, as if watching a movie.

Enough, he thought with a jerking turn of his head.

Tony cleaned up, pulled his workbench to the corner of the room, and covered his materials with a plastic tarp to avoid tempting Penny if she stole away again while Kristen slept. The thought of the Husky being left outside so Kristen could use the bedroom with Ryan without interruption flashed through Tony's mind. Another shot of adrenaline coursed through Tony's system.

He brushed it off and continued to clean up.

When Tony finished, he turned on the downstairs wall lights and locked the front door behind him. Walking around the house, he dropped off his tools in the back of his pickup truck, locking them in the storage trunk, then returned to check on Penny.

When she saw Tony, the animal jumped up and down to celebrate his arrival in the backyard. Was there any more loving being in this world than a dog? He realized she hadn't left the yard all day, having missed her daily walk, scheduled for the evening to tire her out before the long car ride to San Diego.

An idea occurred to Tony. What if he were to take the dog with him? He could take the dog for a run and return her afterward. It would allow Tony to pop back in later to spoil their fun.

At once, he loathed himself for letting the idea run through his mind. *How fucking pathetic do you need to be?* Tony thought to himself.

Penny's joyful kisses came without pretense as Tony knelt to remove the extended leash from her collar but stopped himself. He would make good on the only part of his idea that wasn't pitiful and take the Husky out on a good long run. Tony moved to fill Penelope's food bowl, then stored it in the back of his truck. He then wrote a small note and placed it on the stairs for Kristen.

PENNY WAS RESTLESS. I'VE TAKEN HER WITH ME FOR AN EVENING RUN AND SLEEPOVER. I'LL BRING HER BACK IN THE MORNING. - TONY

As Tony returned to the yard, the animal was again excited to see her favorite human, as if five weeks had passed instead of minutes.

"You wanna come with me?" he asked, receiving sheer jubilation from the lonely pup. "Okay, love, here we go."

Tony attached her standard leash to Penny's collar and walked her to his truck, where she hopped up into the main cabin to sit in the passenger seat. Shutting the driver's door behind him, Tony reached over to roll the passenger window down for his best girl.

A few moments later, the wind was flying through her silver-white fur.

CHAPTER TWENTY-EIGHT

AFTER KRISTEN AND RYAN FINISHED THEIR ROSÉ AT Denner, they left for L'Aventure to drink the syrah and cabernet curveé, then to Turley for the massive zinfandels. When they arrived at Linne Cold for the grenache, the estate's resident Border Collie raced to meet them, thrilled to welcome them to his farm. When they arrived at Epoch for the mourvèdre, a magnificent Norwegian Forest Cat with an untamable black and amber fur coat lay on Kristen's lap to purr his approval. At each vineyard where they stopped, it felt like the couple were drinking in people's homes rather than visiting commercial tasting rooms.

The day had been one of Kristen's favorites, the trip possible only because Ryan's car, with its super-computer at the helm, drove itself between vineyards. Indeed, they were both deep in the bag.

"I haven't been this drunk since my sophomore year at SDSU," Kristen remarked, falling into fits of laughter.

Everything was funny to them this afternoon, and they enjoyed each other like children on a playground.

"All those wine coolers at Beta Date-A-Guy?" Ryan asked.

The very idea sent Kristen's head back into the patio chair with spasms of joy.

"Cheap vodka at Alpha Eighty Proof?" he continued. "No, you're a border-town girl. How about warm Coronas at Lamda Smegma Krappa?

"I wasn't in a sorority. I'm sorry to disappoint you. And it was rare that I partied at school," Kristen answered. "I partied with friends at bonfires on the beach."

"They let you drink on the beaches there?" he winced.

"Of course not," she scowled. "Everyone just holds a soda bottle that's half-filled with booze. Then they act cool in front of the police. It was a perfect disguise. None of us got caught."

"Did you lose it at a bonfire?"

"I got a lot of play at those bonfires, but I lost it in the back of my high school boyfriend's van," she admitted.

"He had a van?" Ryan eyed her with suspicion. "Was it called 'The Mystery Machine' by any chance?"

Kristen snorted and took her time getting through another fit of laughter.

"That's not what he called it, but I believe it was the same year and model," she acknowledged.

"You're joking," he side-eyed her.

"I am not," Kristen insisted. "It was his father's—a light blue Dodge with a custom *Star Wars* poster on the sides. The Millennium Falcon and other ships were flying through outer space. Of course, we got honked at everywhere we went in the damned thing."

"That's so badass! You're like royalty. Did he slip Your Worshipfulness the ol' Han Solo in a Star Wars Mystery Machine? It's almost too much for me to wrap my head around."

"That's what I've been trying to tell you," she nodded. "I'm quite the catch."

Ryan kissed her, the light gesture soon slowing down to become more intense. He had kissed her all afternoon at every place they'd gone. There wasn't a doubt in Kristen's mind how infatuated he was with her. She'd been on the receiving end of many false displays of affection, but this was clearly the real thing. Ryan was too happy and too drunk to be anything but sincere.

The patio at Epoch Winery was lovely but modest, and the couple's intimacy wasn't something they could hide from the other visitors or staff.

"Take me home," Kristen whispered in his ear when she stole back her lips long enough.

"You're dreaming," Ryan snickered. "I can just feel my feet."

"Then you're done," Kristen said and reached for his glass to slide it out of his reach dramatically.

"All right then, if you say so," he smiled, "let's go get it."

Ryan fumbled with his phone and tapped the screen a few times. His car's ignition started from a distance, and the black machine backed out from its parking space. Soon, the vehicle proceeded toward them and stopped near the roundabout.

"Our carriage awaits us."

The setting sun was in their eyes as the Tesla drove them west on Highway 45 back to Cambria. He tuned the radio to an EDM channel, a favorite of Ryan's, which had surprised Kristen. It turned out Ryan was a hard-core electric music festival lover. When Kristen had joked about driving to the desert to stand around in pasties and a thong to listen to DJs "play," Ryan spoke up to defend the ritual, describing every reason he all but lived for those events.

Kristen felt like she was floating within the aggressive, synthesized beats as the car swayed back and forth along the winding road. Its systems kept the car centered in its lane.

Was there anything lovelier than day drinking? Ryan would no doubt say it was a hit of Molly and sand in your ass.

An idea struck her, something she'd seen in a movie, and Kristen was just drunk enough to try. She leaned over and reached to lay her palm on his crotch. The gesture caught Ryan unaware and startled him before realizing what Kristen meant to do. At once, she found him and pulled at the bulge in his pants. Kristen felt Ryan's organ stir, and he pushed himself against her hand.

Soon reaching with both hands, Kristen unzipped Ryan's fly and reached into his dark briefs to pull out his stiffening cock to the light. *Perfect*, she thought, lowering her head to take him into her mouth.

Ryan exhaled at length, breathing a long measure as she lavished her affections on him. Kristen took as much of him as she could manage, the drunken freeness of her muscles daring to accommodate him far deeper than usual. Impressed at tasting his pre-cum so soon, she drew back and reset his organ in his shorts, zipping his fly as if the exchange had never happened. Just a little tease—a promise of what awaited him.

To Kristen's surprise, Ryan trembled. Looking over in astonishment, Kristen saw he was stifling laughter.

"I'm sorry," Ryan giggled. "I can't believe you did that. You know the people at Tesla are recording this, right? A dozen cameras are in here monitoring my eyes and sensing how my hands weren't on the wheel. It's like a voyeur's dream. They probably have a sensor that thinks you were trying to nap on my lap. I'm surprised an alarm didn't go off to warn me."

Kristen didn't have time to become self-conscious or offended before the fits of laughter returned, and she fell back in her chair at the sheer ludicrousness of it all.

Ryan reached to pull her head to him and kissed her wildly on the lips, displaying no concern for the road to enjoy that sweet mouth again.

The light of day was gone when they finally reached Cambria, and they waded impatiently through the evening traffic. The car pulled up to the house, and Kristen let herself out of the passenger seat long before Ryan could open the door for her.

Sex motivated the woman as it seldom had. Kristen took Ryan's hand to lead him up the small hill to the front door with a spring in her step, one that could not account for the wine that pumped through her veins. He would have no opportunity to bail on her tonight.

"Don't drive angry, now. Don't drive angry," Ryan teased, having trouble with the walkway steps as the pair made their way to the front door. Kristen fumbled with her keys, encountering difficulty as she failed to insert them into the lock more than once. When the miserable thing opened, Kristen pulled him inside and found his lips again with a resurgence of excitement, then reached down to stroke his package through his slacks. Even as her mind drifted to find her balance in the spinning room, she couldn't restrain her savage impulses. Kristen needed all of him, and she greedily took what she wanted now, pulling him by his belt behind her to ascend the stairs.

A small sheet of paper crinkled when she stepped on it. Kristen lifted it close and squinted to read the simple two sentences from Tony, which claimed he'd taken Penelope home for a sleepover.

"That lucky bitch!" Kristen exclaimed and giggled as the sheet fell to the side where she cast it.

When Ryan asked what had happened, she didn't bother to answer.

In her room, with the door closed behind them, Kristen lifted his shirt impatiently, stretching the fabric of his polo to rid his body of the wretched garment. When Ryan helped to raise it over his head, Kristen fell to her knees and pulled at his pants to drop them. She brought out his cock, again stiffened by her exertions, and tugged his balls a bit to bring him forward into her mouth.

Ryan exhaled again with delight, gathering his balance by placing his hand behind her head.

"Wait," he whispered. "Wait, babe, please."

Kristen looked up at Ryan, baffled.

"I gotta pee first," he laughed at her expression. "I'm dying. Hold on."

"Me first," she flashed her eyes before pushing him back to rise.

The alcohol erased all feelings of strain, and Kristen flew to the ensuite bathroom.

"Oh, shit," Ryan pleaded. "No, wait, I'm gonna wet myself."

"One minute," she said, shutting the door behind herself.

There was no way she'd let him go first. If she'd learned anything at SDSU, you can't allow a guy to pee first in situations like this. He'd otherwise be fast asleep when she got back to bed.

The act took much longer than expected, but she eventually completed her duty and even remembered to flush and wash her hands. Opening the door, she found Ryan seated on the bed, removing his last sock with more than a little trouble. Now undressed, Kristen saw the tattoos on his upper body.

It's Christmas, she thought with delight.

Kristen pushed him back onto the bed, evincing more

laughter from the bullied man as she ran her hands over his chest.

"Wait, no, you're killing me," Ryan cried as she gripped his stiff cock with covetous determination. "It's already gonna take forever to go down so I can pee."

"Fine," Kristen relented with mock exasperation and rolled over onto her back.

Finding his way back onto his feet, Ryan did a double-step toward the bathroom as if the floor were moving under him. Kristen thought it the cutest thing ever, and she let out another fit of laughter at his goofiness.

Seconds after he'd shut the door, Kristen heard Ryan fall loudly, evoking even more laughter from her. Kristen sat up and undressed when she gathered herself, casting the clothes on the floor. The last thing the poor boy needed now were more obstacles.

When at last undressed, Kristen fell back on the bed comforter, her bare bottom exposed toward the bathroom door. A reasonable calling card, she mused.

Taking his time, Kristen examined her phone while she waited, finding nothing but a list of emails she couldn't be less interested in reading.

A wave of sweet intoxication pulled at her mind, and she smiled, shutting her lazy eyes for a moment.

CHAPTER TWENTY-NINE

THE MAN WAS NERVOUS AS HE DROVE HOME THROUGH the winding roads. Kristen sat behind him, feeling the car lean too heavily as it met each turn. His heavy foot ensured they moved as fast as the compact car could. Several times, he looked at the passenger seat, where his jacket covered a small canvas bag.

Arriving at the house, he pulled the car up the driveway, relying on inertia to push it up to the hillcrest, which the taxed motor couldn't quite manage. The man stood up from his seat, pulling the jacket and cloth bag by its handles.

Kristen moved behind him as they walked up the porch steps to the front door. He looked back at the road, allowing Kristen to see his steel-blue eyes set under his heavy brows. His face startled her. Kristen knew him somehow. The young man was quite handsome, his chiseled face lit up by the golden sun as it set over the clouds rolling in from the Pacific. Anxiety had carved his features with concern, and he turned back to enter the house.

Looking around, Kristen saw the home was only a shell. No one had installed the wainscoting, and the ceiling bore none of the ornamentations she come to associate with the house. Nor had anyone laid the hardwood floor in many downstairs spaces—the roughly-cut underfloor beams exposed.

Kristen heard the man's thoughts for the first time as if he had told them aloud. The house was unfinished because his father, the home's artisan, died before completing its construction. Looking at the materials piled in corners, Kristen realized she observed them through the man's eyes. She was inside his mind. He was ashamed to look at the unfinished work, and the shame mixed with sorrow over how he hadn't the knowledge to complete the work himself.

But that was about to change.

In the kitchen, the man pulled a small parcel from his bag. Wrapped in old linen, he removed the plain wooden box underneath and set the box down on the kitchen counter. After a few deep breaths, he unlatched the flat square box and lifted its lid.

Kristen beheld a circular piece of gold whose perimeter glinted even in the dim overhead kitchen light. When he lifted it from the box, Kristen saw ornate patterns of feathers engraved in the circle, each etched over small ocean waves that moved from the center toward the back. Eight small golden chains fell from the rim, with rubies tangling at their ends.

It was a crown, Kristen realized.

The man held the stunning piece of jewelry with shaking hands. He had stolen it, and the fear of his act would afford him no rest tonight. But no one would discover the artifact was missing. He was sure of it.

His manager told him to lock up everything unidentifiable from the unusual Greek shipments in Storage Shed #5. The curator had tried for weeks to identify its pieces to no avail.

After being pressured to produce results, the curator moved on to the other set of crates. It might be months before those artifacts would see the light of day again. It was the perfect opportunity, and before sealing the shed, he'd slipped the box holding this crown into his bag.

But what to do with it now? He had no black market contacts, and the distributors who might have welcomed such items were far beyond his reach. In the morning, he would search the phone book for antique dealers. They would never give him what it was worth, but it would be enough to hire the contractors needed to finish the house.

But that couldn't be tonight. The adrenaline of the theft had poisoned his body, and he was exhausted. He would hide the artifact until it was time to sell it.

The man returned the crown to its box, his hands almost shaking. He knew where to hide it and walked the box into the living room. Opening the door to the coat closet under the stairs, he pushed aside the hanging garments and stepped forward. He knelt near where the ceiling descended to a small crawl space at the back.

He pulled at a small wood panel to reveal a dark space his father had designed to hold valuables. It was the perfect spot no one would look for, his father had once assured him. Laying the box down in the dark space, he reached to replace the wooden panel, but stopped short.

He wanted to look at the crown one more time. He unlatched the box and lifted the lid, then ran his fingers along the front where the two gold halves joined in an ornamented clasp of bird claws.

The world around him dissolved at once, and the man saw a candlelight-filled room. There were voices all around him lifted in prayer, a low song of reverence by people wearing masks of black feathers. A deep voice spoke a word to him he'd never heard before, but he knew what it meant.

"Slave," the voice said to him.

The young man jumped with a startle, and the closet returned to his sight. He'd been terrified by the vision, the sound of that dark voice echoing in his memory. Panicked, he closed the box lid hastily and shut the panel to hide it in the secret space.

Fumbling backward, he stood up and pushed through the hanging garments to return to the living room. He swung the closet door shut behind him, the slam startling him as much as the voice had.

There was ice in his veins. Chills ran their course through his body as he remained consumed by fear. An urgency to get away from the place took hold of his feet, and he stumbled to the front door. He didn't understand why he fled, but the young man needed to escape.

A terrible force knocked him back before his hand could touch the door handle. It lifted him into the air and pulled him down on the exposed beams of the unfinished floor with a violent slam that knocked the light from his eyes. The pain was all he knew, writhing and pulling at his consciousness.

And then there was nothing more.

The man opened his eyes and sat up to examine the living room. Again, he felt the urgency to leave and rose to his feet. Arriving at the front door, he opened it to find nothing beyond the frame. Though he could see the world through the windows, he saw nothing but a black, empty void when he stood at the open door.

From behind, he heard the bodiless voice again.

"Stand guard, slave," it rumbled.

In a panic, the man turned back to the living room to find the source of the sound, but no one stood behind him. On the floor, just five feet away, he saw the body of a man, his head frozen in horror with his eyes and mouth open, blood pooling around his head and seeping through the underfloor boards.

The face was his own.

KRISTEN AWOKE WITH A STARTLE. THE DREAM HAD been little more than a sense of panic, and as she opened her eyes, the fragments all but left her. Kristen's eyes closed again from the heavy pressure in her head that wanted more sleep.

She felt Ryan's hands massage the skin of her backside with long, possessive strokes. *There you are*, she thought with a smile. Kristen felt his hot breath and wet tongue as he rimmed her with deep licks. The violating sensation shocked Kristen's eyes open, but they soon closed again to feel the stubble of Ryan's face prickle across her skin. His sharp stubble mixed with the intense pleasure of his invasive tongue, and Kristen moved her hips with delight.

Opening her eyes again, Kristen saw her clock read three-fifteen in the morning. It seemed they'd both had a healthy wine nap. It was fine by Kristen, who'd slept just as hard as Ryan had. But her mind was still heavy with the drink, and she closed her eyes, letting the sweet sensation of his mouth tease her bottom.

The tongue bath continued until he found his way to that little nugget of flesh that made her moan with delight. Kristen writhed as he invaded her, flicking and sucking at her sex until the wetness was hers as much as his. Ryan's slid a finger inside her, the hardness delighting Kristen, who rocked and squeezed to hold him. Then a second finger joined, and she was in heaven. Ryan pushed up on her G-spot with one hand and on her pubis with the other to produce a fire that spread through her body.

When Kristen thought she'd lose control, he pulled out and moved to lie beside her. Ryan fell behind Kristen to spoon her, the heat of his body enfolding her frame, his mouth finding her earlobe to suck at.

Ryan slid deeply inside Kristen, and her wet sex stretched to accommodate him. The act sent a flame through Kristen, and she surrendered to the luxurious depth he found. Ryan then cupped her breast, pinching her nipple between his thumb and index finger, teasing it to hardness.

Kristen thought the whole was a perfect mix, and her orgasm was not far away. Ryan thrust eagerly, finding that insatiable rhythm that brought Kristen to cry out as wave after wave of fire spread through her. Finding his own end, Ryan gripped her entire body, and Kristen felt him climax along with her in tremulous fits of pleasure.

When Ryan had exhausted himself, he whispered in her ear with the sound of desperate content.

"I love you so much. Stay here with me," he said.

Kristen smiled to hear his honest plea, and she opened her eyes, the alarm clock's light focusing her eyes. In moments, Kristen felt him pull away, and before she could move to hold on to Ryan, he was gone.

She reached for the switch to turn on the bedside lamp in the dark. Bringing her legs to the ground, Kristen sat up on the bedside. Looking around the room, she couldn't find Ryan, but then noticed the light around the bathroom door frame. He was inside, she realized.

Kristen hadn't noticed if Ryan had worn a condom, and she waited for him to finish so she could use the bathroom. She searched the bedroom floor for her clothes, found her shirt, and slipped it over her head.

When no sound came from the bathroom after another couple of minutes, Kristen's impatience led her to knock on the door. When no answer came, she pushed inside.

"Can I use the bathroom, please?" Kristen implored with a quiet voice.

A wave of rancid urine smell caused her to blink and grimace. Looking at the ground, Kristen saw Ryan's body lying on the wet tiled floor beside the cast iron bathtub, his limbs mangled in an awkward pose that she didn't understand. Beneath his head was a pool of blood, dried at the edges.

On his white face was a frozen look of terror.

THE END

The story continues:

ABOUT THE AUTHOR

Joseph Stone is a historical, dark-fantasy novelist who lives in San Diego, California. He holds a Bachelor of Science in Psychology from San Diego State University and a Master of Arts in Industrial and Organizational Psychology from The Chicago School of Professional Psychology.

To learn of upcoming releases, visit:
WWW.AUTHORJOSEPHSTONE.COM

Follow Stone at:

amazon.com/author/josephstone

goodreads.com/joseph_stone

instagram.com/josephstoneauthor

tiktok.com/@josephstoneauthor

facebook.com/josephstoneauthor

youtube.com/@josephstone3401

Printed in Great Britain
by Amazon

28745759R00137